For Spiros, Makis, Dimitris and Poppy Karaviotis,
Gerasimos Razis-Galiatsatos and Anna-Maria Simpson

Text copyright © Bernard Ashley 2011
The right of Bernard Ashley to be identified as the author of this work
has been asserted by him in accordance with the Copyright,
Designs and Patents Act, 1988 (United Kingdom).

First published in Great Britain and in the USA in 2011 by
Frances Lincoln Children's Books, 4 Torriano Mews,
Torriano Avenue, London NW5 2RZ
www.franceslincoln.com

With thanks to Iris Ashley, Gullë Stubbs and Litsa Worrall
for their help in researching this book

A catalogue record for this book is available from the British Library.

ISBN: 978-1-84780-055-8

Set in Palatino

Printed in Croydon, Surrey, UK by CPI Bookmarque in January 2011

135798642

AFTERSHOCK

BERNARD
ASHLEY

F

FRANCES LINCOLN
CHILDREN'S BOOKS

Chapter One

Shakings and tremblings beneath his feet were as normal a part of life as the hot sun in the summer, goats on the hillside, and shoals of silver *atherina* in the sea. Makis had always known the rumble of the earth, when for a few seconds the land would move like a slight swell under his father's boat. He was used to getting out of his mother's way when he heard a pot crash because someone had put it too close to the edge of a shelf. Whenever he felt the ground begin to shake, he knew how to stand firm, with his feet apart; and if it went on for more than a few seconds, he knew to run outside – or if he couldn't, to get beneath a door frame, or crawl under a bed. He knew that the walls wouldn't wobble all that much, and that while one village had its walnuts shaken from the trees, another village might feel nothing at all. This was life. People on his Greek island of Kefalonia still talked of the horrors of the two wars they had lived through – World War II, and the Greek civil war – but no one talked much about the perpetual war between two tectonic plates deep beneath the Ionian Sea.

So when the earthquake struck that August morning, he wasn't too bothered. At first.

The village of Alekata was made up of ten or so one-storey houses, a small church, and a *kafenío* where the men drank coffee, the buildings all lying along a narrow road above St Thomas's Bay, between the ferry at Pesada and the wide beach at Lourdháta. It was ten kilometres on Makis's father's motorbike from the island capital, Argostoli, where he moored his fishing boat; and with the goats, the olive grove, the walnut trees and the constant sound of the sea, it was home to Spiros, Sophia, and Makis Magriotis. The house might tremble a bit, but it never suffered more than cracked plaster or a fallen vase. It had walls of local rock fifteen centimetres thick, with strong oak beams and a roof of solid, interlocked red tile.

But there had been rumbles for a couple of days, as if a restless underground giant was shifting in his sleep. Adults had begun looking at one other with knowing faces, nodding seriously as they talked in low voices. Makis and his friends knew what all that was about. So many small tremors so close together could be the giant Poseidon waking up to a wall-shaker. His father knew a song about it, which Makis and his mother used to sing with him, sitting under an olive tree at sunset: Sofia mending clothes, Makis reading a book, his father Spiros plucking the strings of his mandolin.

> *'When the ground beneath begins to shake*
> *Beware, beware, beware:*
> *The giant below has stomach-ache*
> *Beware, beware, beware.'*

The first word of something more serious came from Sami, the ferry port on the east coast. In Alekata the tremors had been slight, but buildings had fallen in the east – and the faces of the adults began to look the way they had during the wartime troubles. Things could be working up to something big.

That Tuesday morning, Makis's father brought in his Monday night catch to the Argostoli quayside. There weren't many boxes of fish to unload, not even of the common silver atherina. The sea had been agitated the night before, the lantern at the boat's stern had twitched like a sprite, and the fish had been nervous.

It was a school holiday, so back at home Makis caught and milked the goats – but they were skittish, and somehow the milk seemed thin. In the kitchen, Sofia was mixing red wine with oil to sprinkle over a *horiátiki* salad. When Spiros was back from Argostoli the three of them would eat together.

But he never came.

Finished with the goats, Makis went through to his bedroom to find a towel for a swim in St Thomas's Bay, but as he grabbed it off the chair, his world suddenly collapsed on him. The earth went crazy, the wildly shaking floor threw him off his feet, a terrifying wind howled through the house, and deep beneath him a monstrous thundering roared. There was no time to run outside to the safest place. Shattering into mosaic pieces, the plastered walls fell in upon him, the blue shutters banged off their hinges, the beams lurched, and the ceiling disintegrated as the roof came crashing down.

Makis screamed and rolled frantically under his bed, shaking with fear for almost the full minute that the earth quaked, curled like a hedgehog, covering his head with his arms. Then came a stillness, no sound but that terrifying wind, and no sight but a choking grey dust screening the sunlight coming in through the gaping roof.

Makis was fighting to breathe, drowning in dust. And again the ground shivered. Fallen doorways and broken furniture creaked, and from somewhere outside he heard his mother's voice: 'Makis! Makis!' It was muffled, as if she was far away.

'Mama!' he croaked.

'Lie still! Don't bring down more! I'll get to you...'

And Makis knew that lie still was all he could do. His bed was covered by wall and ceiling and roof. He'd have to tunnel out from here, or do as he was told and wait to be rescued. The dust seemed to be settling. A good coughing and spitting relieved the tops of his lungs; and in a new state of fear he prayed, and lay as still as he could.

At last he heard his mother coming, nearer and nearer, stone by lifted stone. Beams were shifted and tiles thrown. He heard a man's voice, too, but it was not his father's – it sounded more like the priest. They seemed to take forever getting to him. But Makis knew that they could easily bring more of the building down. His father had told him that rescue from an earthquake had to be as planned and delicate as a hospital operation.

Finally, lifting the roof beam that was pressing hard down upon his bed, the priest gently but firmly pulled Makis out by his feet.

Still shielding his head, Makis coughed up powdered Kefalonian rock. He couldn't even get his breath to kiss his mother 'Thank-you!' But he was alive, and uninjured; and she was, too. Now they had to find out what injuries his father had sustained.

But Spiros Magriotis was dead. While Father Ioannis sent Makis and a village girl, Katarina, into the shade of the olive grove, Sofia ran to Argostoli, along the cleaved and cracking road that Spiros would be trying to ride on his motorbike. But he didn't come; and as she searched the waterfront and found his scuppered boat with no sign of him, she ran into the town that stood no more. Fine Venetian buildings were strewn across the roads and the main square; the sewers stank where they had burst, and rescue still went on for people trapped, and for the removal of bodies. It was a place of scream and wail and sudden silence when a whistle blew to listen for sounds of life.

Sofia ran inland to where Spiros usually went

delivering fish, to the Mandolino restaurant. But that had fared badly – and she was called by a shop-keeper she knew to a collapsed building in nearby Kabanas Square – to have a sheet lifted before her, and to see a terrible sight that she would never forget.

No village, no home – and no father any more. That Tuesday morning Makis's life changed from routine and security to an existence where nothing shocked him, and anything could happen. His father was dead. Three of his village friends were dead. The boat was in splinters on Argostoli waterfront and the house a pile of rubble. That night, he and his mother slept with the goats. But at least she was here. She had run outside when the first wind howled, not realising that Makis was in the house. And thank goodness she hadn't been cooking in her kitchen! A mother in the village had been burned alive when their gas cylinder exploded.

For the first few days they lived in what they'd been wearing when the earthquake struck. It was the same for everyone. They herded the scattered goats, drank their milk, and on the third night slaughtered a ram to cook over a fire made from salvaged wood. It was August, so the nights weren't cold; but the chill Makis and his mother felt as they slept under the olives was the coldness of death: of Spiros, father and husband, claimed by what people called an act of God. To which Sofia shook her head, and spat, 'You mean an act of the Devil.'

Help came. A British ship in the area brought sailors and a field hospital and fresh food and water. This was quickly followed by other naval vessels, and villages of tents were set up for the thousands of homeless. Wheelbarrows and carts carried relief along the roads and the tracks where cracks and great holes stopped vehicles from driving; and the churches sanctified nearly six hundred burials, so that gradually their part of the island lost the sickening stench of the dead. But what were Makis and his mother to do with their lives? Makis's only grandparent – whom they rarely saw – lived away north in Fiskardo; she could not support them. Without the boat there could be no fishing. In any case, Sofia was no fisherman; and Makis was too young. Like thousands of others on the island, their way of life had ended. Beautiful Venetian buildings had collapsed into the same common rubble as humble village homes, or stood like decayed teeth in the town's jaw. There was no government building or Mandolino restaurant in Argostoli because there was no Argostoli. There was no Alekata village, either, no church, and no *kafenio* where the men might drink coffee and plan for the future. And although Makis had learnt to play the mandolin from his father, he had no heart to sing Spiros's folk songs. Everything special about the island of Kefalonia had gone.

So it was no surprise to Makis when his mother told him she had taken up an offer from the Greek government to go abroad, to start life again in some other country. And because the first ship to help had been the *Daring* from England, when given the choice for this ship or that, she chose for them both to go to London. Some of Makis's friends went to New York, some to the Greek mainland. Instead, a month after the life-changing earthquake, Sofia and Makis Magriotis boarded the ship for England, and Tilbury Dock, and a Greek-speaking part of north London called Camden Town.

Chapter Two

It was as gloomy as a cave. When Makis looked up out of the window, all he could see were the bottoms of black railings, the tops of the houses opposite, and the grey sky. Ninety-seven Georgiana Street in Camden Town was no Kefalonian house. It didn't stand alone – it was squeezed in a long terrace – and their part of it was almost under the ground, down a flight of stairs from a door in the hallway. Because the small concrete yard at the back was not theirs to use, Makis and his mother couldn't just walk out into the daylight, the way they could in Alekata: it was up the stairs, along the hall, through the front door and out into the street. And far from being warmed by the sunshine of their island, the house was as full of coldness as the ice room at Argostoli market. But their kitchen did have cold running water, which meant no bucket-carrying from a well – one small consolation for being in this English dungeon.

Some of the other residents acted as if these earthquake refugees were lucky to be lodging there. On the top floor, an old woman in black lived alone with her sewing machine, and if ever Makis met her in the hallway, she'd stand against the wall with an arm round her bundle of work as if a look from him was going to dissolve all her stitches. On the ground floor were Mr and Mrs Papadimas. The man worked at Lawford Wharf on the canal, and his wife was a bossy forewoman in *Daphne Dresses* round the corner in Selous Street. Both were Greek-Cypriots, but they might as well have been Turks, going by the friendship they showed. *Daphne Dresses* was the clothing company that was helping Sofia and Makis to settle by giving Sofia a job as an apprentice machinist; but however welcoming most of the other women in the factory might be, Mrs Papadimas wasn't of their kind. She was a woman with a voice like a cracking beam, who'd kept her own bits and pieces down there in the basement before they came – so now she acted as if the Magriotises had deliberately caused the earthquake that had forced her to give up

11

her downstairs space.

Pleasanter sounds came from the middle floor. Walking home from school, Makis could hear piano music and singing and violin coming through the windows. But Mrs Papadimas told him there was to be no noise from children because Mr Laliotis worked in an orchestra at the BBC. He needed to practise in peace, and his wife gave piano lessons in the house. Makis thought it would have been nice, bumping into people who played their instruments as well as his father had done, but Mr and Mrs Papadimas lived on the floor between them, and stared accusingly if Makis or his mother hovered in the passage between the doors.

No longer did Makis go to school on the bus, the way he had in Argostoli. Although the Camden Town school was a long walk away, it was not on a direct route. And after school there was no father to grip him by the arm and say, as he always had when he met him with his motorbike, 'My clever son. Tell me how you made this dunce from Assos proud.'

The schools nearer the house were full, and

Imeson Street School had few Greek-speaking children in it, and not much understanding of Greek ways. There was no translating English words for Makis there, no gentle introduction to the English language. He had to sit at the back of the class, and most of what the teacher said was a mystery, what was in the textbooks just marks on the page. He sat next to a girl who snivelled all the time, so she was no help; and the teacher who set about teaching him to read in English was in the infants' school, where for an hour a day he had to sit with six-year-olds. And to add to everything, there was a Greek-Cypriot boy called Costas who went round telling everyone that Makis Magriotis smelt of goats.

The school was big, too – three storeys high, reaching up like St George's Castle near Perátáta. With its thick walls, from inside the building the outside world seemed far away. But on Makis's third day sunshine spread itself across the playground. Out of pity one of the boys in his class picked him for the dinnertime football match. One team's goal was painted on the wall of the boys' lavatories, and the other was between two posts of the wooden fence at the far side of the playground. No one wore anything special for the game – they all knew who was on which side; and the ball wasn't a real football, it was a scuffy little tennis ball. But Makis soon found that the game was real enough. Even if he had to run round people who weren't playing, and even if there were no throw-ins – just bounces off the walls and fences – in their heads everyone was playing in a stadium. It was real, and it was as serious as the Olympics.

Makis had never been a footballer in Kefalonia. He had fished and swum and wrestled the horns of the biggest goats; but his village had been on a sloping hillside, so playing football on a pitch had never been possible. But he found that he wasn't bad at the game. He was put at the back of the team, to defend: but as the game went on he found himself moving further and further up the pitch; and when the ball came to him, instead of thumping it down the playground like a defender, he kept it at his feet and tricked it round an opponent before he passed to someone who was shouting, 'Mak!'

There was no half-time; they didn't change ends in these dinnertime games; but about halfway through, the boy who'd picked him – David Sutton from the top class – sent someone back to defend in his place and pushed Makis forward. 'Inside-right,' he said – which Makis didn't understand, but when he ran to stand just behind the forwards on the right hand side, Sutton put his thumbs up, as if to say, 'Stay there.' And at the end of the game, when the going-in bell went, Makis got a slap on the back that nearly floored him. 'Good game!' Suddenly he started to feel he belonged.

When the same teams fitted in a quick match during afternoon playtime, he was put at inside-right from the start, and again he did well. In fact, the headmaster, who was on playground duty, joined in the game, and as Mr Hersee was bringing the ball out from near the goal to make a run across the playground, Makis tackled, and robbed him neatly.

'Lucky bounce,' the man said.

'Thank you,' Makis replied, as he passed the ball up to David Sutton.

It was hard to take that happy feeling home with him. His mother, who'd been ruler of the house in Alekata, seemed lost in London. She said the electric sewing machines at the factory were too fast; a slightly-too-heavy touch on the pedal sent everything rumpling on to the floor in a tangle of cloth and thread.

The factory talk was of London things, or of Cyprus, and the jokes were rude; while all the time the overseers wanted more and more 'pieces' to come off the production line faster and faster.

Like many of the women, Makis's mother worked the early shift so that she could be home for Makis after school, which left her with nearly two hours on her own before he came in. But after cleaning their rooms, would she go out for a walk along the canal bank, or to look at the shops, or to sit in the park? Did she try to? No. Afternoon after afternoon when Makis got in from school, feeling pleased with a good pass or a goal, ready to try a new English word on his mother, she'd be sitting in the dim light of the basement window, not even looking out, but with a handkerchief at her eyes.

Had they done right, then, coming to England? Well, Makis thought, it would be better to be here, when the Kefalonian winter winds blew and the rains came, with no money, no work, and only a tent for protection on the island.

'Why don't you go for a walk?' he'd say to his mother. She would go out with him on Sundays after the service at the cathedral in Pratt Street, but never on her own. And he knew why she always shook her head at his question. One afternoon in the first week he'd found her huddled in the bedroom, crying. At first he'd thought she was still grieving for his father – after all, Makis himself dreamed of the man as if he were still alive and living with them here in London. But on this afternoon his mother had carried on crying even when he gave her a kiss, and started shaking as if she was in some sort of shock.

'I went round too many corners. I didn't know where I was. When I asked people the way, they said nothing I understood. I couldn't say the name of this street in English. A man shouted at me, a woman walked me to the police station – but when I saw its big door, I ran.'

'So how did you get home?'

Shivering, she'd shrugged her shoulders, wailed as she had at his father's funeral. 'St Gerasimos. Perhaps St Gerasimos guided me back...'

So now Makis knew why she wouldn't go out without him. His English was slowly getting better through being at school, and he was being slapped on the back for his football in the playground. She was lonely and nervous, scared of being lost in this big place, and went only to the Greek-Cypriot factory and the Greek-Cypriot shops just round

17

the corner from Georgiana Street. Even the patron saint of Kefalonia couldn't be relied upon to guide her home from further afield in north London.

And seeing his strong mother becoming as timid and frightened as a goat for the slaughter is no sight for a son who cares.

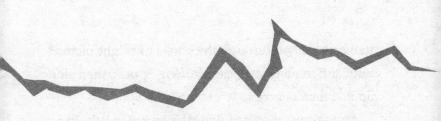

Chapter Three

It was clear that Costas Kasoulides, coming from a Cyprus family, was never going to be a close friend, but they played dinnertime football together and gradually he stopped coming out with the smelly goat stuff: no one thought it was funny, now that Makis was doing so well at football.

In lessons, bit by bit, Makis was moved down from the back of the class, and over into the first column of desks on the right. He was working his way through Gateway Arithmetics quickly because back in Argostoli arithmetic was regarded as important for shipping and navigation, and he'd got further by Standard Five than these London kids. So, for that subject his teacher Mrs Wren was pleased with him. And Miss Prewdon in the infants' school was starting to move him on through the books of bright pictures with different colour names: Red Spot... then Blue Spot... then Green.

Back home, they had done things differently. In his Argostoli school everyone had learnt to read together, all the class chanting the words out loud through the pages of the book, and doing it over and over. Makis had suddenly found he could read on his own. Here at Imeson Street he sat with four or five infants who were on his level, looking hard at the pictures in the books for clues, like the one with a girl riding a red bicycle.

See my bike.
My bike is red.
See me ride my bike.
See me ride my red bike.

Makis found himself moving from one infant table to another quite quickly, on through these books of different colours, where the children in the pages lived in a bright house in a sunshiny place that was nothing like Georgiana Street. Soon he was moved from one infant class to the next one up, and then to the youngest junior class. Better still than his reading, he was understanding more and more of what people said. And now he could write his address in English: his new, dark, London address. His pride on seeing it written down on paper far outshone the gloom of the place.

One Monday morning a special piece of reading in the school corridor made him jump, and smile, and say his new word, 'Crikey!' It was on a notice-board near the staffroom door. There was his name – *M. Magritis* – coming out at him the way his own name always did, as if it was written with blacker ink than the others. And even though it was wrongly spelt, it seemed to do a little dance on the paper.

Team to play at St. Michael's Thursday

R. Hickson   M. Long   F. Gull

G. Tremaine   M. Magritis

C. Kasoulides   D. Sutton   P. Chambers

P. Nichols   E. Brightmore

B. Cooper

It was signed by the headmaster. Boys pushed and jostled around it, until Mrs Wren came out of the staffroom and shooed them into the playground – where, instead of starting a game, everyone stood around and picked the team to pieces. And Makis and Costas were targeted by jealous Denny Clarke from the top class, who'd been left out – because they were in the class below him.

'I play inside-right,' he moaned.

'Till Makis came,' David Sutton told him. 'And you've got a swinger instead of a left foot.'

'I've got a brilliant right.'

'Hersee talked to me about it, an' we both reckon Magriotis is better.' Sutton turned to look hard at Makis. 'So you'd better be all right when we play with a proper football.'

'What this proper football?'

'Leather. Regulation size. Got any boots?'

'Game not here?' Makis waved towards the playground pitch.

Costas snorted, and told Makis in Greek: 'It's a match against another school. Fred Berryman Cup. Four o'clock, over on Prince's Fields. Proper pitch and goals. He won't have boots,' he told David Sutton, 'not coming from his little island.'

'I've got an old pair, too small for me,' Sutton said. 'He can have a lend of those.'

'Which day? When?' Makis interrupted, in Greek.

'Thursday,' Costas told him. 'We walk round to Prince's Fields after school. Get changed, play the game, go home from there.'

'Ah.' And the sun suddenly went in for Makis. What would his mother do if he didn't go straight home after school? The way Denny Clarke was going on about it, getting picked for the team was a big thing, like being picked for the boys' choir in Argostoli. It should have made him feel good, but it was like a seesaw: the more he felt up, the more his mother seemed down.

But Thursday and football went clean out of his mind when he got home from school that day. As he let himself in through the front door and crept quietly along the passage to open the door to the basement, he thought he heard the sound of a plucked string: something musical, coming from their flat. He stopped and listened. Yes. There it was again: a plucked string: not proper playing, but a plucking note. Slowly he went downstairs and opened the door to their flat. There was no one in the living-room; the sound was coming from the bedroom.

He tiptoed across to the closed door. A different string was plucked, and Makis recognised the sound. If it was a G, it was well out of tune; but it was definitely a mandolin – not being played, not being tuned, just being touched.

Was his father still alive? Had they made a mistake and buried the wrong person? Had the British sailors taken Spiros Magriotis to their hospital on the ship, and he was alive after all?

Makis knew it couldn't be true. But then, how was a mandolin being plucked at ninety-seven Georgiana Street?

And now he heard another sound: the sound of his mother crying. Quietly, he opened the bedroom door; and there she was, sitting on her bed, hunched over the instrument. He sat down next to her, put his arm around her shoulders – and saw that it was his father's mandolin. In Kefalonia, mandolins were not as common as balalaikas, but most were lighter coloured than his father's, which was made of reddish wood. And he could see the chip on the right edge of the body that his father had always stroked before he played, as if he was smoothing it down – and the name on the headstock was The Gibson. This was definitely the same instrument, the one his father had taught him on – and all the time they'd been in England, Makis thought it had been lying smashed and splintered beneath the rubble of their house in Alekata.

Makis laid a hand on the mandolin, and stroked the chip on its right side, the way his father always had. 'You're clever to bring this, Mama. How come it wasn't smashed?'

Sofia wiped her eyes. 'It was in its case. Your father always kept it in its case.'

'But everything was smashed…'

'St Gerasimos,' Sofia said. 'He kept it safe. And, afterwards, I wrapped it in the clothes the sailors gave us.'

Makis took the mandolin from her, tightened a couple of strings, and plucked them. He gave it back without a word. 'Then we'll keep it safe ourselves, and I can play it for you.'

But his mother didn't look any happier. He stood up, and pulled her up from the bed. 'Now we're going for a walk. Come on.'

'A walk?'

'Yes. Like Sundays.'

'Where are we going?'

'Somewhere.' He hunched his shoulders as if

their walk would be wherever their feet took them. But he knew where they were going. After getting some directions from Costas, he had a rough idea which way to go to find Prince's Fields, where he was going to be playing football on Thursday after school.

He took her coat from its hook and helped her into it – the evenings were getting chilly. 'Come on. Out to give your eyes something to look at apart from needles and thread. Then we can cook some *pastítsio* for dinner.'

And as he said it, he felt like a father with a daughter. He told himself he wasn't being selfish going to find Prince's Fields. It was all for her, really. If he didn't find ways to lift her out of her gloom, she was going to end up lying on her bed all day, cuddling his father's mandolin.

Chapter Four

On the day, she didn't go to see him play. Although they found Prince's Fields together and he walked his mother there again the following afternoon – telling her over and over how to get there – when Makis and the Imeson Street team turned up for the match on the Thursday, she wasn't there.

But so much was going on that Makis didn't have time to fret. For a start, David Sutton's stiff old boots had to be opened up to let his feet into them, then laced tight. Makis watched how the other boys did it. Stamping and walking, the boots didn't fit too badly, although he felt a year taller with those nailed studs on his soles. Now the big question was: how would he get on with a real football? Would he be the right boy to play at inside-right instead of Denny Clarke – or would he be a disaster?

David Sutton gave him some practice. While Mr Hersee went round talking to the other boys, the captain took Makis and Brian Cooper and a spare ball over into a goal mouth and told Makis to fire shots at the goalie.

The ball was big, made of leather in T-shaped panels, laced up like Makis's boots and smeared with grease to keep it soft. Except it wasn't. It was pumped up as hard as iron, and the first shot Makis took at it felt as if he was kicking one of the bollards on the Argostoli quayside. It hurt, shuddering up through his body and making his neck ache. But he said nothing, and deliberately didn't look at the other boys' faces. He disobeyed the captain and instead of firing another shot at Cooper, he ran about keeping the ball at his feet while he got the feel of it, going round in circles and spirals, steadying it with the inside of his foot, then the outside, poking it ahead of him, until he turned and ran towards the goal, and from the penalty spot he shot the ball at the goal. It went about two metres.

'Sorry!' Makis shouted, and straight away took a meatier kick, this time catching it just right. Cooper was pulling a face at Sutton, and the shot hit him on the cheek and went through between the posts.

'Crikey!' Makis said.

'That's it! Keep going!' Sutton shouted – as he and Brian Cooper with a big red mark on his face ran back to Mr Hersee for his last-minute instructions.

Down at the far end of the pitch, Makis could see the St Michael's boys pulling on their white shirts. But there was still no sign of his mother; so round and round he went, getting more and more used to passing the ball, and shooting towards the goal. Finally, feeling more at home and seeing both teams starting to run on to the pitch, he picked up the ball to join his side, feeling as if he belonged out there in his Imeson Street red vest.

St Michael's wore proper white football shirts with school badges on, and black shorts and long socks; while for the Imeson Street team it was their dyed red vests that were the same. Their shorts were different colours, they played in ordinary socks, and Makis wore his school short flannels with a snake belt to keep them up. But a black coat doesn't make a priest, as they say in Argostoli. St Michael's looked the part, but Imeson was the better team.

They played twenty-five minutes each way, with Makis getting more and more used to the size of the pitch and the strength needed to pass the heavy ball. At half time – two goals up by David Sutton – Costas explained the Cup Match to Makis. 'Today's the first round. If we win, we play another winner in the second round, then another school's team in the quarter finals, then another team in the semi-final. Then, if we win all those, we play in the Cup Final in Regent's Park. And if we win that, we've won the Cup, and we keep it for a year.'

Makis knew where the Cup would go on show: but how many matches would they have to play before they could put it in the glass case outside the headmaster's office? Would they all be after school? And would they all make his mother feel bad because he'd be home late? He counted in his head. If they won this, there would be four more matches to play – four more unhappy afternoons for his mother.

'What happens if we lose?' he asked in Greek.

Costas blew out loudly. 'We won't lose!' he said. 'We're two-nil up already.'

'But what if we do?'

'That's it. We'll be out of the Cup.'

'And no more matches?'

'Only if Hersee can fix up a friendly.'

Makis looked away, and tightened the laces of his boots. Apart from going to the nearest shops, his mother wouldn't leave the house without him; she didn't speak enough English to trust herself on her own. How miserable would she get on Thursdays, week after week, if he didn't go home straight after school? How unhappy was she right now – probably crying on her bed and cuddling his father's mandolin?

It was a strange thought, but wouldn't it help her if the school lost this match today?

Mr Hersee blew his whistle to call the teams back on to the pitch. The other school's PT teacher had refereed the first half, so now it was his turn. Running up and down, would he notice if Makis played badly? Makis had never cheated like that in his life and his stomach twisted with the shaming thought.

It took him a while to get used to playing in the opposite direction. With his first touch of the ball, he didn't pass it up the pitch to Freddie Gull, but back down the pitch to Ernie Brightmore – and the angry yell he got from Sutton told him the team would never forgive him for playing badly. So he had to choose between his unhappiness or his mother's – and right now, selfishly, Makis didn't want it to be his. Out there among the boots and legs, all he could think of now was winning the game, of how well he could do.

With St Michael's defending more strongly, relying on their big centre-half to whack the ball up the pitch, it grew more difficult to thread the passes through, a challenge Makis was enjoying. This was what he was good at: collecting the ball, running it at his feet, beating a player or two, and putting a good pass out right to Gull, or left to Kasoulides, or up to Sutton. He didn't shine. He didn't score. But he didn't play badly and he wasn't a traitor. And as he came off the pitch with the game won at 4–0, he threw himself on to the grass with the others, a happy body in the heap of congratulation. Although not brilliant with the big ball, he felt he deserved his place in the team.

'Through to the next round! Well done!' Mr Hersee said. 'Next Thursday, let's see who we get.'

Next Thursday. Makis's celebration froze at the reminder of his mother back in Georgiana Street. For an hour or so this afternoon, he had felt like a boy who lived in Camden Town, instead of an earthquake survivor from Kefalonia. But for now, this was the end of feeling good. He'd had his ration of being up.

She had been crying again. She was cooking meatballs

in the kitchen, trying to look bright for him, but he knew she was putting on a show. Her smile wasn't much more than a quiver of the lips and she couldn't disguise her eyes.

Makis told her about the game, and said nothing about her not being there. He gave her his red vest to wash for next week, and he showed her the boots that Sutton said he could keep until they'd won the Cup. She nodded – but she could no more show pleasure than a fish can look alive out of water. It was how she was: sad, and growing ill. He remembered that illness from back home in Kefalonia. Some widows were strong and carried on for ever. But Makis had seen others in their black dresses and headscarves behaving like this; their bodies bending when they had been straight before, wailing on feast days instead of singing. And what happened next? They died, and people said how happy they were, together again with their husbands in heaven.

And now his mother was going that way. It hadn't happened straight off; it was more of an aftershock, like the tremor following an earthquake. He could see signs of her getting ill in the head. Yes, that was what lay in the future, unless he could do something about it.

Chapter Five

The idea hit him when he was in Miss Baker's room.
This was the youngest junior class, where instead of
being at an infants' table Makis was squeezed with
two other boys along the seat of a wooden desk,
each taking a turn to read a line from a page of their
reading – the Green Spot book. In it, Sally, the girl in
the Colour Spot stories, was sitting with her mother
on the grass in a sunny garden.

"Read to me, Sally.
Read to me from your book.
Do you like the story?
Is the story good?"

As the lines were read, what was happening in Sally's garden jumped out at Makis. Sally was being helped by her mother, the way Makis's parents had always helped him with his school work. They already knew the things Makis learned at school, and went over them with him in the evenings. So why couldn't he and his mother do the same, but the other way around? Why couldn't he help Mama to learn English the way he was learning it?

'Come on, Makis – it's your turn to read!'

"Yes, the story is good," said Sally.

The next boy took over, but Makis stayed concentrated on what he was doing. He didn't want Miss Baker to think he wasn't getting on, he wanted to make progress, to catch up with the children in his his own. From now on – and his mind was made up – he was going to learn English for the two of them: for Makis Magriotis, and for Sofia Magriotis, too.

He deliberately missed the start of the morning playtime game in the playground. Today he was on a mission, a secret mission. As soon as he was out through the door, he turned round and ran back inside, as if he'd forgotten something. Silently he skirted the school hall, hurrying past his own classroom, and came to the double doors that would take him into trouble.

He stopped. These doors were the crossing point between the juniors and the infants, doors he'd been allowed through up until the week before. But he didn't go to the infants' classes any more, so if he was found along the infants' corridor, he couldn't just pretend he'd left something behind. And he'd been in the school long enough to know where he was and wasn't supposed to be; even today, standing up in the hall with the football team in morning assembly, he'd been reminded of it. Before the football announcement Mr Hersee had complained about stealing from the cloakrooms and the serious punishments it brought. Going through these doors could put Makis in big trouble.

But this morning he'd had that good idea – and the thought of it gave him courage. Things were bad for Mama at home, and he had to do something about it.

He pushed through the doors.

Everything was nearer the floor on this side. In the cloakroom the long seats for changing were almost at ground level, and the slipper bags all hung low – beneath coat pegs which had fruits and animals on them instead of names. It was easier to be seen – but, high or low, there was no one about. Stealthily he crept along the corridor, keeping close to the classroom walls. It was a dry day, so all the infants would be out in the playground, their teachers in the staffroom, and he'd be all right if his luck held out. *If.* His heart thumped as he imagined a teacher standing silently behind a door, ready to step out and catch him. He felt so scared and out of place that he wanted to turn back, to get out to the game he could hear being played in the distance. But he was driven on by thoughts of his sad mother. Makis Magriotis had come into the Infants' School for something, and he was going to get it.

Mrs Carew's classroom was the last in the corridor, and the nearest to the Infant teachers' staffroom. Makis wouldn't have long to carry out his plan; morning play lasted fifteen minutes, and the teachers went out a few minutes earlier ready to line up the children; so he had to move fast. If someone came out of the door, he could ask for what he wanted. The trouble was, if the answer was 'no', he was stuck, because then they'd know what he was after.

But the staffroom door stayed closed, and when he passed the first classroom, no one came out. He came to the second classroom door: and again nothing happened. He came to the third classroom door: and – *help!* – there was Mrs Young over at the far wall, pinning pictures of sailing boats to the display board. *Don't look round, please!* He crouched beneath the glass in the door and hurried on towards Mrs Carew's classroom, the last in the line. The door was open, and Mrs Carew didn't come out.

He could hear the teachers in the staffroom, talking and laughing. Now for it. Quickly, he slid into the classroom and ran to the tall stock cupboard over by the window, hoping that it wasn't locked. Like a wardrobe, it had two doors, and as he tried the nearer door it opened. *Yes!* He swung it fully open to give himself cover and looked inside. And there they were, a neat stack of Red Spot books, and a neat stack of Blue Spot books – the first two in the series, the books he'd gone through before being moved on to Mrs Young's class. Quickly he took one of each and pushed them up under his jumper, holding them there with one hand. Now to get—

'What's all this?'

It was Mrs Carew, at the classroom door! Makis was hidden for the moment – she wouldn't see him straight away. But she could see the cupboard door was open when it shouldn't be. He went cold; his throat tightened and he wanted to swallow, but he couldn't – it would make too much noise. He was well and truly caught, like a lobster in a pot. Mrs Carew would see him with the books up his jumper, because he dared not move a muscle to put them back. No school books were allowed out of the school building.

He held his breath and listened for her footsteps.

'I said, what's going on?'

It was then he realised she was still out in the corridor.

'Showing us all up, working through playtime? I brought you a cup of tea…'

Makis squinted through the crack of the cupboard door. Mrs Young was there with Mrs Carew.

'If I didn't get those pictures up, they'd be so disappointed. They were from yesterday afternoon,' Mrs Young said.

'Drink your tea, Val. I'll bring your class in.'

'You're a friend.'

More like an angel sent by Saint Gerasimus! thought Makis. As he watched, the stolen books getting dangerously slippery in his hand, Mrs Carew went off towards the playground, and Mrs Young went back to her own classroom.

That was close! But Makis was far from being through those double doors and back in the Juniors. The other teachers were coming out of the staffroom, and he still had to get past Mrs Young's door.

He stood there. He sweated. He'd got himself into a deep, deep, hole. If he got caught, no matter what punishment Mr Hersee gave him, no one would ever trust him again.

Suddenly boldness paid off. Boldness and luck – the luck of seeing Mrs Carew's milk crate of empty bottles over by the classroom door, and the boldness to pick up the crate and carry it along the corridor towards the Junior hall, where the top class monitors put them every day at dinnertime.

Makis never knew if Mrs Young saw him go past her classroom – he didn't look to find out. Instead, he walked with a purpose: to get those Colour Spot books safely out of the school. To start teaching his mother how to read English.

Chapter Six

Makis thought hard about the way he was learning to speak English, the fact that he was with a lot of English children all day. Words rubbed off on him like the lichen off a tree trunk. It had started on the ship coming over. While his mother and the other grown-ups stayed in their quarters, he had wandered the decks and the corridors. He'd grown friendly with the crew members, who taught him things like 'Hello!' and 'See you!' and 'Get your backside out of it!' At first, in the school playground, the most usual phrase he'd heard was 'Clear off!' And in the classroom, when a teacher was pleased, it was 'Good!' or 'Excellent!' Listening to people and talking to them was the important thing.

So that was how he would start with his mother. Instead of talking Greek to her all the time, he would sometimes say things in English, so that at least she could hear the words being spoken. That hadn't been happening at home, or at *Daphne Dresses* with the other Greek and Cypriot women. Then, after a bit, he would start reading the books with her, and point out to her things in the street: signs, notices, advertisements. Some of these were the same advertisements that had been on walls in Argostoli, so straight off, he'd known what *Persil washes whiter* meant. It probably washed whiter all over the world.

But an idea came to him as he walked into the living-room and saw the mandolin – a brilliant idea. At Imeson Street they sang a song: 'Ten Green Bottles'. He could pick that out on the strings. What made it a useful song to sing with his mother were the numbers in it – which he could use his fingers to show. And that afternoon, as he walked into the living-room with the Colour Spot readers under his coat, he felt proud of his idea. His mother had saved his father's mandolin. Now he would use it to start saving her.

She was in the kitchen washing the floor. The floor was never dirty. Only two rubs each way with the wet cloth and it was covered, and Makis knew it would have been washed once already that afternoon; but she had to keep finding herself something to do. In Alekata there would have been a hundred things keeping her busy: making goats' milk into cheese, knocking nails into split fish boxes, netting olives, knocking down walnuts. Each afternoon, when Makis got in from school, she would smile, pour him juice or cold water and offer olives and cake before getting on with her work. But always, she would smile.

Not like today, when she hardly looked up, but sent suds scudding across the stone floor.

'Hello, Mama,' Makis said, in English.

'Hello, Makis,' she replied in Greek.

'Say hello in English,' he said.

'Uh?'

'Say "hello".' He made a handshaking gesture. 'Hello.'

She looked at him as if he was mad, and with a *tchk*, she turned back to the popping soapsuds.

'Hello… Goodbye…' Although she wasn't looking at him, Makis made the handshaking gesture again, and he waved goodbye, before adding in Greek, 'I'm only speaking English tonight.'

But his mother shrugged over her wet cloth, as if to say, 'What silliness is this?'

'I'll make you laugh,' he said. 'Laugh. Ha-ha!' – although he now had his doubts whether even miming falling off a wall ten times like the green bottles would raise a smile on his mother's face. He kissed the top of her head and went back into the living-room.

The mandolin was hanging on the wall like a decoration. Sofia Makis had removed a picture of fierce-looking cattle and put the Gibson in its place. Hanging there, the instrument seemed to please her. Now Makis took it down, and like his father he first stroked the chip on its body, before holding the mandolin to his chest in the position for playing. And, there, at that moment, he felt himself swelling, growing – with a sharp pang in his stomach, as if his father had just walked into the room with his eyes twinkling and his mouth making that *Oh, yes!* pout he'd always made when he was proud.

Makis's fingers went to the headstock, bringing the mandolin up to his ear and turning the A string tuning key. As he plucked and tried to imagine an A in his ear, he took the mandolin as far as he could from the kitchen because he didn't want his mother to know what he was doing just yet. He opened the basement window to the street and sat close to it, hoping that the sound of his tuning would escape like a trapped fly. He tightened the A string up to something near pitch – or his memory of it – and when he was happy with it, he put his finger on the seventh fret and sounded the E, the way his father had taught him. Now he could tune the top string.

But he hadn't got the E up to where he wanted it before a quiet tap came at the basement door.

Who was that? No one ever tapped at their door: Mrs Papadimas only ever rapped, knuckle-hard. His mother hadn't heard, so he went to the door and opened it.

Mr Laliotis was standing there stroking his grey beard, wearing his black cap and a velvet jacket; and hanging from his shoulder was an instrument case on a leather strap, about the size of a violin.

'Hello. I hope you will excuse me.' He spoke in Greek.

'Yes?' Makis didn't know if he should ask Mr Laliotis into the living-room; but with his mother on her knees washing the kitchen floor, he decided not to. In Kefalonia she would have wanted to put on a clean dress for anyone coming into their home.

'Just now, as I was coming in, I heard – I thought I heard – mandolin. It's got a sound all of its own, mandolin.' Mr Laliotis was smiling.

Makis said nothing, but nodded politely.

'I haven't heard it in this house before. You've been in London for some weeks, but I haven't heard such a sound up till now.' He patted his instrument case. 'You see, I am a musician.'

Makis nodded again.

'And it was not just plucking. It was tuning. I'm sure it was proper tuning I heard.'

Makis felt shy. He knew Mr Laliotis played in an orchestra on the radio. His violin was heard all over England; perhaps all over the world. An important man was saying this to him!

'It's a Gibson,' Makis said, quietly. 'It used to belong to my father.'

'Ah.' Mr Laliotis nodded. He shuffled his feet as if he was about to go. 'You must come upstairs some time. You and your mother. We can make some music together.' He leant forward for a final word. 'I don't just play violin. I have a balalaika too.'

'Thank you, sir.'

Mr Laliotis went back up the narrow stairs protecting his violin case from banging against the wall. Makis quietly closed the door, and looked towards the kitchen – where his mother was standing in the doorway holding the top of her overall across her neck as if she was only half-dressed.

'Saint Gerasimos!' Makis said.

'We can't go, Makis. Not upstairs to them. We are country people, and they are very cultured…'

And at that moment, for the first time ever in his life, Makis felt ashamed of his mother. Wouldn't his father have gone upstairs to Mr and Mrs Laliotis to make music? Of course he would. Hadn't Spiros Magriotis sat at the top table of musicians in the Mandolino restaurant on Saturday nights, singing and playing for some of the most important people in Kefalonia?

Makis went over to the window to pick up the Gibson and hang it back on the wall. He would have to forget 'Ten Green Bottles' and he would have to forget the Red Spot and the Blue Spot books: they would have to stay where they were, hidden under the cushions.

His mother wasn't ready to be helped.

Chapter Seven

Makis half-hoped that the team sheet for Thursday's Cup match would not have his name on it. Denny Clarke could play, then Makis would get home at the proper time. But it was only a half hope, because that other important half of him – Makis the boy, not Makis the son – thought it was great to be a member of a team.

And on Tuesday there his name was, in the team on the notice board: the same boys picked as before. At playtime, this was the way the team lined up. They didn't pick sides in the usual way, but played first eleven against reserves – with a moaning, foul-tackling Denny Clarke as captain of the second eleven. He was listed this week by Mr Hersee as a reserve who would walk to the match with them, but once the game started, he knew he wouldn't get to play – whoever was injured, whatever happened. Those were the rules of football.

'Why should I walk to Prince's Fields?' he growled, 'if you're all there?'

'You could give us a cheer,' David Sutton told him.

'I'll give the Greek a kick where it hurts! He's rubbish! Hersee only picked him because his house was bombed.'

Makis decided not to hear that. There were things to fight, and things to let go. He wasn't sure whether or not 'bombed' meant the same thing as 'earthquake' in English, so he left it at that – he didn't want to look stupid. And they all knew that what Clarke said wasn't true about his football. He hadn't been brilliant in the first proper match they'd played, but he'd done quite well, and he was getting better all the time in the playground games. More and more, the team was feeding the ball through him because he did unusual things with it; and he was looking forward to doing it on Thursday at Prince's Fields – as a schoolboy, and not as the son of Sofia Magriotis.

On Tuesday evening he persuaded his mother to walk out with him again to Prince's Fields, piloting her as they went.

'Look, we go past the cathedral, past the street of *Daphne Dresses*, we turn right here...' He marked the corner for her by the big Coca-Cola poster on the wall which said, *Have a Coke!* He was tempted to point out the words in English and tell her they meant the same as the words in Greek. But catch one tuna at a time; in the end, he just drew her attention to where they turned right. It would be enough if he could persuade her to walk to Prince's Fields on Thursday.

It was cold, and not many people went out for walks – the pair of them needed the duffel coats the English sailors had given them. But that was how Makis treated their walk – as a sunset walk towards the setting sun – until Sofia started shivering and said she wanted to go home.

'OK, we'll go back. Mama – see if you can lead me home. I'm not going to say anything. '

'Am I a child?' she asked, looking cross, 'or sick in the head?' She thumped the heel of her palm against her forehead. 'No, I'm not!' And right then, Makis realised what a difficult Red Spot pupil she would be.

But she did lead him home – she wasn't stupid. He made sure he didn't say, 'There, you can do it,' because the way she was behaving tonight, she'd just have shouted at him. He was pleased inside, but he would have to be as clever as Mrs Carew or Mrs Young with the reading books, if he was going to save his mother from herself.

Within a week, Prince's Fields had become a different, wintry place. Everyone was shivering – and Denny Clarke sloped off home at kick-off with a look at Makis that was meant to turn him to ice.

The game was played on a hard, cold pitch – against Hawley Road boys who were hard, cold players. Running in strange boots on a frosty pitch jarred Makis, and the tendons in his arms sent twitches up and down. But Kefalonia can have some hard winters, too – and Makis was a boy who in the past would have gone out in his father's boat when ice .was creaking all the ropes and the cold stuck the fish to your hands. Also, a boy who can dodge a charging goat can easily get out of the way of a Hawley Road defender intent on kicking him up in the air.

Makis's style of football suited playing against a rough side. He wasn't big, and although his arms were strong from wrestling goats and hauling heavy nets, he couldn't boot the ball as far as some of the others, so he kept things tight, made short passes, running on and calling to get the ball back, then sending it somewhere else. And he used what he'd learned in the playground – how to make passes with the outside of his foot as well as the inside – so that a hulking defender would come in at him expecting the ball to go left, then see it going right and lose his balance.

The game was tight, and muscle gave Hawley Road a dubious goal when keeper Brian Cooper caught the ball and their centre-forward shoulder-charged him over the line, which their teacher allowed.

That was the score at half-time: nil-one. But after a word from David Sutton, Mr Hersee pulled a stroke. He told Makis to switch positions with Gordon Tremaine, who was at inside-left. 'Keep those side-foots going,' he told Makis, 'across and forward to Tremaine, and you both send balls to the wings – with Gull and Hickson running in.' He added a touch of assembly-time poetry – 'Slink between their tree trunks like wolves in a forest' – which in plain language meant: use guile and speed and close control against these hefty foulers.

And Makis set up the equalizing goal. David Sutton had just been floored by the Hawley Road centre-forward – although Mr Hersee didn't whistle for a foul, having just given three on the trot – but Sutton managed to knee the spinning ball to Makis, who instead of controlling and using it, took a chance and met it in the air, volleying it out to Hickson on the left wing. Ray Hickson ran in and as the keeper came for him instead of the ball, shot early and slotted it between his legs.

Goal! Mr Hersee spun on the spot and whistled as if he were a referee at a Wembley Cup Final.

Sleeves were rolled up on the Hawley side. Socks were rolled down by Imeson Street. But the hero was Mr Hersee. With two minutes to go, as Michael Long went for a header in the Hawley box, out came their keeper and clattered him – long before the ball arrived. What would the ref do? The most likely answer was nothing, because the ref would be favouring his own team. But he blew his whistle. Penalty! The playing decision was easy; it was the ref's ruling that was brave. And on the dot of twenty-five minutes, after Sutton had scored the winning goal, Mr Hersee emptied his lungs blowing the final whistle. Imeson Street was through to round three.

Makis realised, as he walked home steaming-hot in the cold, that the next game could be played anywhere – even a bus-ride away if Imeson Street wasn't drawn at home. But he was too pleased with taking that chance when the ball spun off David Sutton to start fretting yet. He could have tried to control the ball and pass it short – but that volley had split the other team's defence. And he could still feel the warmth of Mr Hersee's pleasure after the game. He hadn't said anything, but he'd ruffled Makis's hair – and Makis hadn't had his hair ruffled since his dad died.

His mother was cooking snapper when he got in, not fretting in the living-room – so perhaps she was getting used to him coming in late on Thursdays. When the meal was over – with the two of them still at the table – Makis brought out what he'd been sitting on: the Red Spot reading book.

'Mama, please will you help me with this?' he asked. He was far above this level now, but he put on a puzzled look as he opened the book.

'What is it?'

'My reading, in English.'

She looked at it. She frowned. But she was still Sofia Magriotis, Makis's mother, who had always helped him back in Kefalonia.

'All right – after we've cleared the table.'

And then the pretence began. Setting the Red Spot book between them like two pupils at a desk, Makis opened the first double page.

I am Sally.
I am Mum.
"Hello, Sally."
"Hello, Mum."

Makis could read the words perfectly, but his fingernail grooved the page beneath them as if he couldn't. His mother tried to mouth the words with him, then he slowly went over them again with his mother joining in. He turned the page.

I am John.
I am Dad.
"Hello, John."
"Hello, Dad."

After one go-through, Sofia read the page with him, the two of them saying the words together.

Makis risked one more page. This idea of him needing help seemed to work, but he didn't want to keep going on until it didn't. He had to be patient. He would always remember how one summer his father had tried night after night to catch a large grouper lurking in the bay. He had used this bait, he had used that – but most of all, he had used patience. And on the fourth night he had come home with the grouper in his arms, heavy, with a dorsal fin that scraped the lintel of the door as he carried it through. There was a look on his father's face that couldn't be bought for silver or gold.

So Makis would be patient. For tonight, they'd do just one more page.

"Hello, John," said Sally.
"Hello, Sally," said John.
"Hello, Dad," said Sally.
"Hello, Mum," said John.

'Thanks,' said Makis. 'That helped me a lot.'

'Good.' His mother turned to the front of the book and looked through the three double pages again, the words on the left-hand side and the pictures on the right – of a sunshiny garden with trees, under a blue sky.

'Aaah!' she sighed.

'I'll wash the plates,' Makis offered. He wanted to move things forward, not back. Back was too sad.

And at the sink, he couldn't help feeling pleased with himself. He'd helped to win a football match, and he'd got his mother saying words in English!

Chapter Eight

Even Denny Clarke's jealous spite couldn't take away Makis's glow the next day. The Cup match result was announced by Mr Hersee in assembly. The Head's pride was the school's pride, too, and some of the children dared to cheer.

'We do not boo, we do not cheer at Imeson Street,' Mr Hersee admonished. 'We clap, like English gentlemen.'

'Magriotis isn't one!' Denny Clarke growled. 'Dirty little Greek!' He came out with insults in the playground every time Makis touched the ball. 'Dirty Greek! Dirty Greek!' But Makis didn't let them get to him. The others, led by David Sutton, were shouting encouragement at him, and in the end Denny Clarke shut up.

No one could take away what had happened the afternoon before: Makis had been one of the team that had scored a David and Goliath victory. He was beginning to feel at home in Camden Town. And his reading in English was moved on to the Purple Spot in the lesson after dinner break. He couldn't ask for much more.

But when he got home, more was given to him.

After their meal, again he asked his mother to help him with his reading – and she read with him the first three pages of the Red Spot book. He hesitated before he read the first *Hello*, and she said 'Hello' before he did. Then they moved on to page four.

"I can run, John."
"I can run, Sally."
"See me run, Mum."
"See me run, Dad."

Makis's mother stayed silent as Makis painfully spelt it out – but she joined in with him as he tried to speed up, to make more sense of it. And it was while they were doing this – heads touching, minds together at the age-old task, that Makis had his next big lift.

It came with a knock at the door.

'Forgive me for intruding.' Mr Laliotis said.

'Of course.' With Kefalonian courtesy, Sofia gestured for him to come in.

He glanced around the room. 'You are working...?'

Sofia looked at Mr Laliotis, then at Makis, who was holding up the Red Spot book for their visitor to see. And, lifting her head, she said, 'Makis is teaching me to read English.'

Makis nearly fell off his chair. *What?* Was she saving face for him – or had she guessed what he was doing? Had she worked out that he was tricking her into learning English? Whatever it was, he could only smile like a good loser.

'Well, I don't want to interrupt such a worthy enterprise...'

So did she feel OK about learning to read English? Or was this just to let him know that she had seen through him? Some footballs go where you want them to go by bouncing them off a player's legs.

'...However, my wife is out this evening, and I've dusted off my balalaika. When you've finished, perhaps Makis would like to come and rehearse a tune or two?' Mr Laliotis looked at the mandolin hanging on the wall. 'The Gibson *looks* good, but it always sounds even better.'

And Mr Laliotis, the famous BBC violinist, knew his name!

'We'll read the next page, and then he can come up to you. Thank you.'

'And another time, we'll make it a little party, eh? When Mrs Laliotis is at home…?'

But Makis's mother was vigorously shaking her head, and shrinking a little, back into the other, sadder Sofia Magriotis. 'Thank you, but I don't go out,' she said.

Mr Laliotis rode over the refusal like a gentleman. 'That's very sad. But it would give me pleasure to play balalaika tonight,' he said. 'Is it all right for Makis to come?'

'Of course.' Sofia Magriotis was a Kefalonian lady. 'I'll send him up.'

'Thank you. Then for the moment I'll say… ' and here Mr Laliotis smiled, and with a look over at the Red Spot book, finished in English – 'Goodbye.'

To which Sofia bowed her head, 'Goodbye,' she said, also in English and very matter-of-fact, as if she'd been saying it all her life.

Mr Laliotis's flat was everything that Makis's wasn't. It was high above the street, it was light, and it had matching furniture. Where Sofia and Makis walked on linoleum and mats, Mr Laliotis had carpets; and while Sofia and Makis had one armchair, up on the middle floor there was a long sofa and two armchairs. But it was the piano that really set the places apart. It was a baby grand, near the window where the light fell across the keyboard. Makis stood in the doorway and felt like a delivery boy wringing his cap in his hand.

'Come in, come in!' Mr Laliotis had swapped his jacket for a short-sleeved pullover, his bow-tie for a collarless shirt. And in his hands he was holding his long-necked, maple balalaika. 'Let's tune our instruments, eh?' He took the mandolin from Makis and plucked the E string. He then plucked the first of his three balalaika strings, also an E. 'That's not bad!' The tuning Makis had done downstairs brought a little nod from the man, and a wink as he began to tune the other strings of both instruments. 'Please check it,' he said to Makis, handing back the mandolin. It was perfect, of course, and Makis found himself doing that same sudden uplift of his face that his father had used to do, to say that he was ready. But he didn't have a plectrum, and a mandolin needs a plectrum.

'Here.' From a small leather pouch Mr Laliotis took a couple of plectrums, held them in front of him, and handed the smaller of the two to Makis.

'Makis, do you know, "The Cuckoo Sleeps"?'

Makis nodded. Of course he did. Every child of three knew the bedtime lullaby; but the way Mr Laliotis pronounced the title, it could have been one of the classics. 'So, how about if you play the D chords? I'll bring you in.'

Makis set his fingers on the E and G strings and checked the sound with a couple of strokes of the plectrum. He looked up again – to see that Mr Laliotis was now wearing a serious BBC face, the professional musician giving respect to his instrument as he played a concert introduction to the simple tune. In came Makis with his D chords, picked rhythmically across the strings like the tick of a clock. And as they got into the tune, they both began to sing.

"The cuckoo sleeps on the hills, and the partridge
in the bush;
And my baby sleeps in his cot to fill his soul
with slumber."

Only pride held back Makis's tears. At one and the same time he was his father playing mandolin under the olive tree, and the small boy he had once been, hearing the words of the lullaby.

They stopped. 'Will you take the melody now?' Mr Laliotis asked. Not *can* you, but *will* you? And Makis thought he could – in fact, he knew he could. It was simple.

'So…' Again Mr Laliotis did the fancy introduction, and with a nod to Makis, he dropped to the chords while Makis took the tune. And again they sang the lullaby.

'Bravo! Well done!'

Makis was pleased with his playing. He rested his father's mandolin across his knees. No, not his father's mandolin – *his* mandolin, inherited from his father. Makis Magriotis's Gibson. His lips quivered, which he quickly turned into a smile; because if he hadn't, he'd have burst out in a mixed-up wail.

Chapter Nine

Makis was disappointed when the next round of the Fred Berryman Trophy was drawn. Not by the team they had to play – Larkson Lane was a name that meant nothing to him – but by being drawn away at Chase Fields, Kentish Town – not even in Camden. Makis should have been proud to know he'd been picked to play; instead, he wanted the name on that team sheet to be Denny Clarke. But it wasn't, and Denny looked at it and swore when he saw the note underneath: Reserve to travel: Clarke.

'Dirty Greek! Comin' over here an' taking the place of a proper English boy.'

'How do we get to Chase Fields?' Makis asked Costas.

'Get a bus after school,' Costas told him. 'It's a good long way.'

Under his breath, Makis said a Greek word that he shouldn't have known. The game was on Thursday next week. What was he going to do? Tell Mr Hersee he couldn't play? Or work on his mother, prepare her for him being extra late that evening? Well, he didn't know right now, so he just had to leave things as they were.

The problem went out of his mind when he walked in on her. She was sitting at the table with a Red Spot book. It wasn't open, but it was there – and somehow her face seemed different. The no-hope look wasn't there tonight. Instead, she looked the way she'd be on a bad day in Kefalonia, not a bad day in Camden Town. There was a world of difference.

'Are you going to help me again?' he asked.

She gave him a look, as if to say, *who's fooling who?* He broke away and warmed his hands at the electric fire, rubbing them enthusiastically, the way his father always did when he saw his favourite meal on the table.

Like a girl in school, Sofia opened the Red Spot reader at the first page, and even as Makis was pulling up a chair she read from the beginning with hardly any prompting from him. It was only her accent that was different from a London schoolgirl's. So now there was no pretence. She wasn't helping him – he was teaching her.

They came to the next new page.

"I can jump, John."
"So can I. I can jump, Sally."
"See me jump, Mum."
"See me jump, Dad."

See you jump off Mount Énos! Stupid kids! Makis thought. But after helping his mother with a phonic sounding-out of *j-u-m-p*, he was delighted with the way she raced down the page. In his chest he felt a teacher's pleasure, thinking how she was going to enjoy *The Man Who Ran to Sparta* when they got to it. He'd enjoyed it best of all the books when he'd read it himself. It was a proper Greek story.

Sofia finished the Red Spot book, and with a flourish Makis pulled the Green Spot book from behind his back.

'Red,' Makis said in English, tapping the first book. 'Green.' He pointed to the colour of the second. 'Like the traffic lights. Red and Green.'

His mother nodded patiently. Yes, she understood.

The green book started with Sally in a sunny garden, standing in a small paddling pool: *"See me in my pool, John."*

Sofia looked at the picture and put the back of her hand to her mouth, the way she used to laugh at her husband's jokes. 'See me get eaten by a giant squid!' she said in Greek. 'Silly girl!' It was the first time Makis had heard her chuckle since sunnier times.

He laughed, too. 'No, squid, wait till John gets in the water. Get two together!' Sofia gave a little squeal – and on an impulsive surge, Makis went to the kitchen and brought back a green bottle of cleaning fluid. There wouldn't be much sensible reading done for a bit. He unhooked the Gibson from the wall and, with his fingers finding the right chord, he put a foot up on his chair.

'Bottle,' he said in Greek, pointing to it. 'Bottle,' he repeated in English. 'Green bottle.' He showed her how it was the same colour as the big spot on the cover of book. Now with his free hand flashing five fingers twice, he told her, 'Ten.' He showed where nine imaginary bottles were standing beside the real one. 'Ten green bottles.' And he started on his song:

'Ten green bottles hanging on the wall,
Ten green bottles hanging on the wall,
And if one green bottle should accidentally fall – '

he made the bottle drop over, just a little way –

'There'll be nine green bottles hanging on the wall.'

'Nine,' he said. 'Nine.'

Sofia looked a bit puzzled, so he started singing again, *'Nine green bottles hanging on the wall…'*

And on he went with the song, knocking the bottle over at the end of every verse. Nine, eight, seven, six… She probably didn't understand 'hanging on the wall', but he would come to that later. Meanwhile, he was strumming the mandolin strings and Sofia was picking up the tune and joining in with the words. Her mood was definitely up, and with the sound of the mandolin still in their ears, Makis suggested they leave rescuing Sally from the giant squid until the next day. She smiled as she put the bottle away; and riding the moment, Makis told her about the game coming up at Chase Fields. His mother nodded OK – not overjoyed, but not pulling a face, either.

Wasn't it peculiar, Makis thought, how something

good could come from nowhere and pull you out of a hole?

Denny Clarke reminded Makis of something – and on the day of the match, when he saw Clarke staring at the altered team sheet in the corridor, he realised what it was. He had seen fish looking like Clarke in his father's nets: big staring eyes and a pouting open mouth. Clarke's hair was always stuck close and shiny to his head as if he'd just been fished from the sea, which made him a real brother to a *barboūni*. As Clarke read his name on the playing team sheet, he looked like a red mullet. Paul Chambers was off with flu, so Denny Clarke wouldn't be the travelling reserve after school today – he'd be playing.

Chapman played at right half, which meant that Clarke would be behind Makis – and as soon as playtime came, David Sutton made them practise in those positions. But Clarke annoyed Makis from the start.

'Why don' you drop back, Greekie,' he kept saying. 'so's I can overlap you?' All the same, he stayed too close, crowding Makis; he wanted to be where Makis was all the time. Clarke was bigger and should have fitted better into the half-back line, but he just didn't try – and that wasn't a good sign for the game that afternoon against Larkson Lane.

Even Mr Hersee saw it. He must have been watching from his office window, because out he came. 'Clarke!' he shouted. 'Dennis Clarke!'

'Wha'?'

'Drop back. Keep in line with your centre-half.'

'The Greek kid gets in my way.'

'And you, Magritis – ' the man still hadn't got hold of Makis's name – 'be aware of what Clarke's trying to do.'

'Yes, sir.' It wasn't worth moaning about Barboūni Boy. There'd be more space for keeping out of his way on the big pitch, wouldn't there?

Mr Hersee paid the fares, and they all went on a double-decker bus to Chase Fields, which was different from their Prince's Fields home ground. The goal posts were round instead of square, and they had nets up. Instead of changing under a tree they changed in a council changing-room, and as Makis ran out on to the pitch with its fresh white lines, he suddenly felt smaller. It was a big-time game, all right.

This being a quarter-final, a teacher from another school was going to referee.

It started at a cracking pace. The ball was pumped up hard and it travelled fast, causing mistakes all over the pitch by both sides. But the teams soon settled, and Makis could see how Larkson Lane was different from the teams they'd played before. For one thing, this team had a real coach. Mr Hersee liked football, but he wasn't the same as Mr Laliotis with music or Mrs Pardew with reading. David Sutton said he'd never even played the game. But these Larkson boys had a master who was shouting at them the whole time, telling them where to run and when to drop back. In his football shirt and goalie's cap he bullied, raged, scorned his players, while Mr Hersee in his suit and glasses was just a high voice calling, 'Well done, Sutton', 'Bad luck, Magritis', 'Keep at it, lads!' and, 'Come on, the Reds!'

Another difference between the two teams was that Larkson Lane had been taught their positions as if they were First Division players. Imeson Street were more playground juniors who followed the ball wherever it went. It wasn't just Denny Clarke crowding Makis against Larkson Lane, it was everyone crowding everyone else – until one long ball from the Larkson defence found their left-winger waiting in a park-full of space. They didn't score – but it was clear that like this they would soon go a goal up.

Imeson Street was out-manoeuvred all the time – but not always out-played. When, from a scrimmage, the ball suddenly came to Makis, he went on a run with it, and if Denny Clarke had had his wits about him Imeson Street could have got somewhere. A big left-half came charging at Makis, who was going to get flattened whether the boy won the ball or not. But if Denny Clarke had been Paul Chambers following behind him, what Makis did would have worked. As the tackler's shoulder came heaving in, there was just a split second for Makis to step over the ball and back-heel it. But Clarke wasn't there. He'd run up inside Makis on his left as if it was a race; and when Makis picked himself up off the grass, there was the Larkson left-half running with the gift of the ball towards the Imeson Street goal – where his forward line was in formation for a slick tap-in.

One – nil.

It wasn't all Clarke's fault, it was Makis's as well – he should have been more sure someone was following to collect his back-pass – but it was rotten missing a good chance on the break to go one goal down.

'Bad luck, lads – but we'll come back second half.'

David Sutton saw the problem better than Mr Hersee, and he told the team what they'd got to do. 'Backs stay back, half-backs only up to halfway except for corners and free kicks; and forwards and inside-forwards – we keep our shape: the "W".' He eyeballed his team. 'Stop chasing the ball all over the pitch!'

'Exactly, lads,' said Mr Hersee. 'Hear-hear, Sutton. The "W".'

He drew a quick diagram in the back of his diary, showing the normal line-up of attackers as printed in match programmes.

Hickson   Long   Gull
     Tremaine   Magritis

And with a lot more shouting between the players on the pitch – 'Keep position! Stay there!' and more from Mr Hersee, who started running the touchline from end to end until he was exhausted – Imeson Street got back into the game. They'd got the ball skills, it was the match skill they hadn't mastered, until David Sutton had spotted what was wrong. And by not chasing the ball all over the pitch and keeping their shape better, they competed well – and in the end got a goal back through a sizzling left-wing centre from Ray Hickson that Micky Long chested into the net.

One – one.

The Larkson coach shouted his throat inside out as the teams lined up again. 'Balstock, you idiot – don't leave that winger all that space! Get inside his shirt! Fewtrell, what the hell were you doing? Sit on that scorer – take him out of the game! I don't want to see daylight between you backs and those forwards!'

'Play up, lads!' shouted Mr Hersee from the other side of the pitch. 'Come on, you Reds!'

It was tense, it was tough, and with the teachers trying to move the players around like puppets, it was stalemate: two good teams cancelling each other out.

But David Sutton wasn't finished. Making a clearance, accidentally-on-purpose he booted the ball hard and long off the pitch so that Mr Hersee had to run eighty yards to get it. Urgently, Sutton called the Imeson Street attack together.

'We're getting nowhere like this. Do what QPR did the other Saturday. Forget the "W". We go for an "M".'

'An "M" – what's that?'

'A "W" inside out. The two wingers and Long drop back, and inside-left and inside-right go up. They're marking us one for one: they won't know how to mark us then…'

By now, the ball was back on the pitch. Steered by Sutton, Makis and Tremaine went forward to become the front line of attack, and Hickson, Long and Gull dropped back to play just forward of the half-backs. And the captain was right. After yelling for a few minutes, the Larkson coach went quiet as he tried to work out what to do. But before he could, Sutton's ploy paid off. With the Larkson full-backs drawn too far forward, still sticking tight to the Imeson Street wingers, there was suddenly a space for a looping clearance by Nichols up to Kasoulides on the left – who passed a clever ball through to Tremaine upfront, who jigged about and beat their centre-half – to slide the ball under the diving keeper.

'Goal!' shouted Mr Hersee.

'Offside!' shouted the Larkson coach.

Solemnly, the neutral referee had the ball thrown

to him. What was he going to do with it: place it for an offside free kick, or give the goal?

Without a word he ran to the centre spot and made a note in his referee's notebook.

One – two.

'Three minutes to go!' shouted Mr Hersee in the loudest voice Imeson Street had ever heard from him. *'Three minutes!'* – for the benefit of the referee.

'Right – everyone back!' David Sutton instructed. 'Micky Long, you stay up, in the middle on your own. The rest of us back!' And with a look at the Larkson touchline, he shouted, 'Get inside every one of their bloomin' shirts! I don't want to see no daylight!'

Copying the other side's tactics, Imeson Street hung on by dogged defending. The Larkson's coach could shout 'Four minutes!' when there were two, and 'Three minutes!' when there were none, but the referee blew his whistle on time – and the Reds were through. Imeson Street was in the semi-final of the Fred Berryman Trophy.

And Makis went home late, but elated – to find another sort of line-up on the kitchen table.

Chapter Ten

'Saint Gerasimos!'

Makis's mother had put ten bottles in a row on the table – not all green and not all the same size; but ten, anyway. There was the cleaning fluid bottle, pint and half-pint milk bottles, a medicine bottle, a lemonade bottle, a stone hot-water bottle, a bottle of sauce, an eye-drop bottle, and one full and one empty jam jar. Makis's face lit up when he saw them, with his mother standing to one side as if she'd had nothing to do with them getting there.

'They look like the school team!'

'Ten green bottle,' Sofia said.

Makis counted them aloud in English, putting a finger on each. 'One, two, three, four, five, six, seven, eight, nine, ten! Now you say it with me.'

Which she did.

He went to the wall for his mandolin, and tonight he used the new plectrum. With a quick tune-up – and satisfied with less than perfection so as not to lose the moment – he found his chord and began strumming. And they sang the song, Sofia in a stronger, more certain voice today.

With smiles and some doorway-dodging, they put the bottles and jars back in their places, and after a meal of toast and sardines they spent a serious hour on the Green Spot book. Sofia went through it well, even if she did make the English words sound more like Greek. This was excellent! And because the more advanced Colour Spot books could be found in the junior school, Makis wasn't too worried about getting hold of them to keep up their lessons.

His pupil was doing well; which had to say something about the teacher, too.

The following Sunday morning, Makis and his mother went to the Cathedral; and on the way back, the hoarding at the corner of the High Street caught their eye. It was advertising Canada Dry Ginger Ale.

Makis recognised those four words in English. They had the same meaning as on the advertisement back home in Metataxa Square.

'Look at that!' he said. 'Canada Dry Ginger Ale.' Then he said it in English.

What would his mother think? Would seeing the advertisement from the past make her sad, or—'

'Canada Dry Ginger Ale,' she said in Greek. And repeated what he was saying in English – 'Canada Dry Ginger Ale' – with understanding in her voice.

Makis showed the palms of his hands, like a conjurer after a trick. Perhaps he'd be a teacher one day, if he couldn't be a fisherman.

What a different atmosphere the house had!

Mr Laliotis was given a smiling welcome when he came later that morning; and he was geniality itself. His white hair was fluffed up like a maestro, and in Sunday mood he wore a woollen pullover knitted in geometric patterns – eye-catching enough for Makis to stare at.

'I wear it for the Greeks!' Mr Laliotis said, waving at the designs. 'Isosceles, Euclid, Pythagoras!'

'Mathematicians,' Sofia said.

'I wondered if Makis might help me,' the musician went on.

But how could Makis help Mr Laliotis? It wouldn't be fish boxes he'd want scrubbing out, the way Makis had helped his father; and he wouldn't be hauling in a full net.

'Mrs Laliotis is organising a musical evening at the Acropolis restaurant. She's going to play piano. Together we shall play a violin and piano duet. The men will sing, and I shall play balalaika. But...'

But, what?

'I remember a song from Kefalonia that speaks to all Greeks of their homeland.' He looked hard at Makis. 'I wondered if you knew it from your father?'

He could ask my mother, Makis thought, but for some reason he's asking me. 'What song is that, Mr Laliotis?'

'Do you know, "To Taste the Assos Honey"?'

'Oh!' Sofia gasped, and made a small sound in her throat. She looked as if sadness had come in through the door like a winter wind. 'Spiros...'

Makis jumped in quickly. 'Yes, I know it.' People kept bees all over Kefalonia, but the bees from Assos produced the best on the island.

'Then please will you come upstairs with your mandolin and help me?' Seeing Sofia's sudden look of sadness Mr Laliotis seemed embarrassed, but with a jut of his chin he went on. 'Please?'

Makis looked at his mother.

'Of course you must go,' she said.

Makis went upstairs feeling that he was on two missions at once: for Mr Laliotis, and for his absent father.

Mrs Laliotis was there today; but instead of being third musician, the tiny woman stayed mainly in the kitchen where she was cooking. From time to time Makis could hear her humming along quietly.

After tuning their instruments and a short practice with 'The Cuckoo Sleeps', Makis found the pitch and a starting chord for 'To Taste the Assos Honey', and slowly he picked out the notes of the chorus – making mistakes, going back, correcting – but finally, putting confident words to the island song.

I cross the blue Ionian Sea,
the blue stripes flying at our stern,
but when my sands are running out
to Kefalonia I'll return
to taste the Assos honey.

'Bravo!' Mr Laliotis had joined in as Makis went on. 'Again.' And together they played the chorus once more, bringing it up to something like its proper tempo.

'Well done!' came from the kitchen.

They worked on the first and then the second verse; and after Mrs Laliotis had come in to play the notes on her piano keyboard, Makis wrote the words of the verses and the chorus on a sheet of music paper.

'Sweet and simple!' Mrs Laliotis said. 'The Acropolis is going to be delighted when Yiannos performs this beautiful song.'

'Yes.' And thinking of his father, who had never performed but simply played and sung, Makis was suddenly overwhelmed by sadness, the way his mother had been when he'd found her cuddling the Gibson mandolin.

But in his moment of sadness, he realised how well she was doing, slowly pulling herself up from that deep unhappiness.

It was Makis's week of weeks. In the classroom it was easy to ask to be a book monitor and to hide the next few Colour Spot readers in his desk. School books never went home. They were stamped with the London County Council stamp, counted often, and called 'stock'. History and Geography and Nature Study books were given out for each lesson and checked back into the cupboard by monitors, but readers and arithmetic books were always being changed in the different divisions of the class. So in his desk, ready for his mother, Makis had hidden the Orange Spot and the first of two Colour Spot Story Readers – *Robin Hood* and *The Man Who Ran to Sparta*.

Sofia was keen to go on with the series. In Kefalonia, she'd never pulled a face at anything because it was new. Makis knew boys whose mothers wouldn't listen to new singers on the radio or buy a modern style of dress. They were the 'old' village – as much part of it as the ancient stone houses. But Sofia Magriotis would always try new things – just coming to England to make a new start showed the kind of person she was. So for the past couple of weeks she'd been doing her homework like a student who wanted to get top marks. And now, how about that second story book – *The Man Who Ran to Sparta*? Wouldn't she love a good Greek story?

And the same week, although Makis hadn't played brilliantly in the matches so far, he was picked to play in the semi-final of the Fred Barrowman Trophy. With Pearson back at school, Denny Clarke was chosen as reserve to travel, giving him another excuse to shout abuse.

'Rotten Greeks! All over Camden Town like a plague of rats! Magriotis gets to be teacher's pet just because his house fell down. Well, so did mine, in the war – but my mum didn't push herself on other people.' After the team sheet had gone up, Clarke made so much fuss in the corridor that Mr Davies came out of the staffroom and sent him to stand in the hall during playtime – which gave Makis a little lift. And for the first time, seeing his name on the sheet didn't make him feel all mixed up. He might not go home afterwards to ten green bottles on the table, but he was pretty sure he wasn't going to find his mother crying in her bedroom.

It wasn't often that several sides of his life looked up at the same time. Back in Kefalonia, he might have had a good day in school, and in the afternoon he might have dived for an octopus among the rocks for his mother to fry – but then he'd drop a fish-cleaning knife overboard and he'd be scolded. But this week in Camden Town, even Mr Laliotis was giving him a boost.

That night, with his violin case still tucked under his arm, he came to invite Makis upstairs for a rehearsal of the Kefalonia song. And after a good session, with Makis's fingers surer and surer on the mandolin, he quietly dropped a big surprise.

'You know, I think you could play this with me at the Acropolis.'

What? Makis could only sit there and stroke the small chip on the Gibson.

'I mean it. Our two voices, with mandolin and balalaika – they'll be a special item at the concert. This old man, living here a long time' – he lifted his balalaika to identify himself, the way musicians do – 'playing alongside the newcomer from a tragic island…'

Hearing this, Makis wondered if he should lift his mandolin. He didn't, because Kefalonia might be tragic now but it hadn't always been, and one day it wouldn't be again. But what an honour! To perform a duet with a man whose BBC violin was heard all over the world! To play his father's mandolin with such a man! How proud Spiros Magriotis would have been. His pride would have lifted those Argostoli stones from his trapped body and freed him…

With tears in his eyes Makis said, 'I'll do it, if you think I can.'

'Oh, I think you can. Certainly. Just keep those fingers supple, exercise them, protect them – musicians have a duty to their hands – and at the Acropolis we're going to make a few men cry.'

Like me, Makis thought – but they would be happy tears, because he was so proud for his father.

Chapter Eleven

The semi-final against Griffin Road that Thursday was on the same pitch at Chase Fields. Makis thought Griffin Road must have played against a few easy teams in the Cup so far, because they weren't all that good. And Imeson Street might be playing in dyed vests, but the Griffin Road team turned out in any old shirts and blue team bands, with the captain wearing them crossed – as if it was a games lesson. But nothing could detract from the way Makis played against them. From the start, all David Sutton had to shout was 'W' or 'M', and Makis and the other forwards would switch their formation and have the Griffin Road boys tied up over who was marking whom, chasing the ball about and tripping over in confusion.

And somehow the size of the ball, the fit of his boots, and the passing with both the insides and outsides of his feet all felt natural to Makis. He obeyed his captain, but he wasn't afraid to do his own thing. He'd never felt so much in control. He was the player who saw where the openings were – and calling for the ball, he made the best of them. Even with most of the Griffin Road team surrounding him, he could beat the tackles today and make the passes that scored goals. He didn't score himself; he didn't need to, because whether it was in a 'W' or an 'M', or a chase-the-ball 'S', the game was easily won, five-nil.

'Well done, the Reds!' shouted Mr Hersee; and he made the team shake the hands of all the Griffin Road players. 'First time Imeson's ever been in the final!'

'Good luck to you,' the Griffin Road teacher said. 'You've got a good little inside-forward there.'

'Magritis.' Mr Hersee *still* hadn't got Makis's name right. 'Greek lad from one of the islands. I've been bringing him on, nurturing the boy.'

'Well done. He'll probably win the Cup for you.'

And Mr Hersee walked over to shake Makis by the hand – *actually to shake his hand, man to man.*

Sofia didn't think much of *Robin Hood,*but she worked hard at the words. She thought the story was strange – all that hitting people with long poles and shooting arrows all over the place.

> *Robin was on top of the castle wall.*
> *The moat was down below.*
> *His men were in the boat.*
> *"Come up!" Robin called.*
> *"Come up by the rope."*

Sofia read it with Makis. 'Huh! Jump off, stupid Robin,' she said. 'Make a splash. Fly like Icarus!'

They both laughed. 'The next book's different,' Makis told her. 'You're going to like it.'

> *'The men went to the wall.*
> *They went in the boat,'*

she read.

'Very good!' She was showing some of her old spirit. But they soon put *Robin Hood* to one side, and from behind his back Makis produced *The Man Who Ran to Sparta*. Sofia's eyes shone at the sight of the cover – which showed the herald Phidippides running across rocky ground. Makis knew she'd enjoy learning to read even more if the story meant something to her.

'Do you remember this story?' she asked him. 'I used to tell it to you as a little boy, the way my mother told it to me.'

Makis nodded. He'd remembered it all over again when he was reading the book at Imeson Street. The famous runner Phidippides was a Greek hero – and Makis had imagined himself a hero, too, as he'd read it. It had made him feel that he had his own Greek place in the world, no matter where he was living. The world was a lot bigger than Denny Clarke's Camden Town.

'Shall we start?' he asked.

But there was no reply; and when he looked round at his mother he saw that her eyes were welling with tears.

'Tomorrow,' he said. And he whisked the books away, while Sofia went quickly to the kitchen to wash some vegetables under a noisy tap.

91

Makis was in the team for the Cup Final. He expected to be, after that handshake from Mr Hersee, but earthquakes do happen, and worlds do get turned upside down, so he couldn't be sure until he saw his name on the notice-board in the school corridor. All the details of the match were there today: the date, the time, the team they were against, as if Mr Hersee had decided that this match was important enough for a full sheet of paper instead of the usual half-sheet.

The Fred Barrowman Trophy Cup Final

Team to play against Garland Avenue
on Saturday 6th March at 11 am in Regent's Park

R. Hickson   M. Long   F. Gull

G. Tremaine   M. Magritis

C. Kasaoulides   D. Sutton   P. Chambers

P. Nichols   E. Brightmore

B. Cooper

Reserve to travel: D. Clarke

Meet at school at 9.45 a.m.
New team jerseys will be provided before the day
to be ironed and brought with shorts and boots.
Spectators welcome

And pinned to the wall next to the notice-board was a red shirt from a sports shop, still in its boxed creases. The next morning Mr Hersee gave a talk in assembly about it – 'Pride in the School Colours' – holding up the new shirt.

'Bet he's only bought ten,' Denny Clarke moaned. 'If anyone don't turn up, I'll 'ave to wear an ol' vest.'

Makis stared at the shirt again. Its smell of newness was special. It made him catch his breath, and he was sorry it had been taken down to be shown in assembly. He wouldn't admit it, but every time he passed by, he made sure he got close enough to sniff it.

Saturday morning the sixth of March! Cup Final! Makis knew his mother wouldn't be going to Regent's Park to see him play, but he'd tell her all about it afterwards – and perhaps somebody would take a picture of the team, if they won. It might even be in the paper. And…

But he stopped himself thinking like that. Apart from an old grandmother in the north, there was no one back in Kefalonia to send the picture to, and that would have been the best bit of it – buying two or three copies of the paper for the village friends he no longer had.

Chapter Twelve

The red football shirts were given out to the team during Friday assembly, when the twelve players on the teamsheet – including reserve Denny Clarke – were called out to the front. Mr Hersee presented the shirts with two hands as if they were military honours. And when Makis got his, he only just stopped himself from giving it a good sniff.

'Take these home and wear them tomorrow with pride!'

Brian Cooper the goalie didn't get a new jersey – his old green roll-neck jumper would have to do. And Denny Clarke had been right: he didn't get one, either. The looks he gave Makis as the school sang 'Glad That I Live Am I' poisoned the meaning of the joyful words.

'Eleven o'clock tomorrow, Regent's Park. Imeson Street will be in action.' Mr Hersee waved a hand at the line of players as he jutted out his chin. 'Let's have a good turn-out to support the lads.'

And that afternoon, Makis ran home with his face buried in the brand-new Cup Final shirt in Imeson Street red.

The night before the big match he hardly slept. He kept touching the shirt lying folded on the chair beside his bed. In his head he passed the ball with the insides and the outsides of both feet, and in a glorious jiggling run he beat four players before slotting home a cunningly deceptive winner. But that was day-dreaming; he turned this way and that, trying to get off to sleep and mostly, he turned to the red shirt side; but he was still awake. Why were nights so long? Why couldn't life be all days without these great waits in between? He wanted to be at Imeson Street, meeting up at ten o'clock for the team bus journey to Regent's Park – not having to lie here in bed.

In the end, he was deeply asleep when he felt himself being shaken.

'Wake up, Makis! Wake up! It's half-past nine.'

He was woken by his mother – but what mother was this today? It wasn't the Sofia Magriotis who had bravely brought him to England. It wasn't the woman who had found ten green bottles to line up on the living-room table. And it wasn't the laughing woman who had invited a giant squid to jump up at Sally in her paddling pool. It was the red-faced and tearful mother Makis had found clutching his father's mandolin, weeping and rocking herself in her bedroom those weeks back.

'What is it?' He forced himself up to see his mother clamping a hand across her mouth as if she dare not speak. *'What?'*

She turned her face away and went from his room. He got out of bed and followed her. She had been cleaning. Three cushion covers, ready for washing, were hanging over the back of a chair. The ornaments from the mantelpiece were on the table, lined up for dusting, next to the small pile of Colour Spot readers ready to be returned to school, closed and in their proper order. And lying there, too, was the book his mother was working her way through – *The Man Who Ran to Sparta*.

'What is it?' he asked again.

'Get yourself washed,' she said. 'Just look at the time.' The mantelpiece clock on the table said nine thirty-five. 'You're never this late waking up. What time have you got to be at the school?'

'Ten o'clock.'

Makis started dodging between the scullery outside and the kitchen as he gave himself a quick wash – while his mother filled a kettle, cut two slices of bread and put them under the grill. She threw an oilcloth across the table and set down a plate, all the time keeping her face turned away from Makis, bustling about as if everything was normal. Makis knew it wasn't, though – and this was suddenly proved by a huge hiccup, the sort that comes from nowhere after tears.

'Mama! Something's the matter – what is it?' He wanted an answer, but he had to keep going, drying himself and looking for his trousers.

She burnt the toast. His tea wasn't poured. Pulling on his trousers and cramming his football boots, shin pads and the new red football shirt into a bag, Makis tried to move round in front of her, face to face. But it wasn't easy. She scraped the toast outside the back door, she buttered it standing against the cooker. She was hiding her face from him, and she wasn't going to tell him what this unhappiness was all about. So Makis went into the living-rooom to the book that she'd been looking at, lying upside down but open on the table. *The Man Who Ran to Sparta*. He turned it over.

And now he knew. He remembered this page from when he'd read the book himself, in school.

The picture of the runner's face at the end of his run – the only real close-up – looked like someone he knew; someone he loved. Phidippides was very like Makis's father – the same thick, dark hair, the same thinnish face, sharp nose and crinkled eyes. It could have been Spiros Magriotis there on the page, except that this man was in pain, his face screwed up in terrible anguish. During her tidying, Makis's mother must have let the book fall open right here. Now, the sudden noise she made behind him was like an animal in pain. She reached over and grabbed the book to close it. But he wouldn't let her.

'Is it this?' he asked her. 'Tell me… What is it about this picture?'

She stopped struggling with the book and stared at him. 'He looked like this. Your father. When they pulled the Argostoli stones from on top of him. I saw him before they…' She couldn't go on.

This was something Makis had never known about, had never dared even imagine. He knew a lot about the day of the earthquake, but there were gaps.

He hugged his mother and she hugged him back; but he wasn't comfort enough for her. All her bravery – in coming to England, in working at a factory job she hated, in learning to talk and read in English for the sake of their new life – all this seemed to drain out of her at the sight of a picture of her husband suffering. With a wail, she slumped across the table.

'Mama! Mama!' Makis felt helpless. He ran to the kitchen and brought a cup of water. He put his arms around her shoulders. 'Drink this.'

She lifted her head to take a sip, spluttered and coughed, and racked her thin body. She stared at Makis and put her knuckles to her mouth. 'What he must have suffered! Not a mark on his head or face, but suffocated, his body crushed…' She closed her eyes and leaned her head on Makis's shoulder, who held it there for a long time until slowly, slowly, she began to calm down.

'I'm sorry,' she said. 'It just… caught me…'

Makis released his grip. To think that this was the book he'd brought to please her. And with his insides churning, he heard her words again and felt the pain of his father's death. Not the pain of the fact of his death – Makis was always feeling that, but the terrible understanding of how much his father must have been hurting to make his face look like the runner's in that picture. He imagined the agony of being buried by crushing stones, fighting to breathe beneath a fallen building. Poor man! Poor Papa!

Sofia was trying to pull herself together, to put on a brave face, but she looked as lost and alone as a child without friends in the playground.

'What… time… is it?' she asked.

But right now, Makis didn't care what time it was. Cup Final or not, he wasn't going to leave his mother in this state. He must stay with her until he knew she would be all right on her own. Wasn't that what his father would have done?

Chapter Thirteen

'Makis! It's your football match! You've been picked. You can't let your team down.'

With a steadying hand on the table, Sofia pulled herself up straight and became his mother again. And when a mood like this overtook her, there was no ignoring it. 'Get yourself to school!' she ordered him.

The clock said nine forty-five, and he needed twenty minutes to get to school, even running. He had to hope Mr Hersee didn't march the team to the bus at ten o'clock sharp. He tore himself away from his mother and, grabbing his bag, ran up the stairs, out into the ground floor hallway, and frightened the old woman in black from the top of the house – who flattened herself against the wall. In seconds he was outside and pelting along Georgiana Street towards the crossroads.

Please don't go on time, Mr Hersee!

Why can't people in the street walk in straight lines? And why do they have to suddenly stop to look at nothing at all and get in your way? He crossed roads, he dodged cars, he swung his bag and accidentally knocked it against a woman's leg.

'Oi! Watch out!'

'Very sorry.'

He didn't slacken his pace. He pushed on at top speed like the man who ran to Sparta, hot, out of breath, his legs aching, and his heart thumping – to turn the last corner into Imeson Street, and see the school closed. 'Oh, crikey!' There was no line of boys fidgeting just inside the gate like before. The gate was already locked. The caretaker had vanished. They had gone. They had left to catch the bus to Regent's Park without him.

So now he had three choices. He could run to the bus stop. He could go back home, but that, he knew, was not a choice. Or he could run as fast as he could to Regent's Park – except that he didn't know the way.

He chose the last option: he would ask someone. He turned on his heel and ran to the main road where the buses ran. Phidippides couldn't have run harder. He stopped for a gasp of breath and asked a man,

'Regent's Park? Which way? This road?'

'That's right, son, Pancras Road. And when it stops being Pancras Road, go right—'

But already Makis was pelting along the bus route on Pancras Road – in too much of a hurry to hear the man finish, 'go right on'. He ran past one bus stop, past another – until, looking up with sweat in his eyes to check the road names, he saw that Pancras Road stopped at this next junction and became Crowndale Road. What had the man said? *Go right when Pancras Road stops.* Makis took the turning to the right, and he suddenly recognised where he was. This was Royal College Street, and it led back towards his own home! He would have to run the length of it and ask again.

Running to school and coming back to being level with his own street was like running from Alekata to Lourdhàta. Already he was exhausted. Even if he got to Regent's Park in time, how could he ever kick a heavy leather ball after this?

It was up at Camden Road that he asked the way again – and the woman he asked looked at him as if he was mad for not knowing the way to Regent's Park.

'It's down there, i'n it? 'Course it is. Down there, past your underground station, and straight on till you 'ear the lions!'

The lions? Makis had heard talk about a zoo in Regent's Park but he'd never been there, any more than he'd been to the park itself.

Every step was harder than the last. Now he really was like Phidippides – at that point where the hero had run beyond exhaustion. He could well understand how the runner came to drop down dead at the end. But Makis pushed himself on – past the World's End pub, past the Spread Eagle – and what he'd give to see the sea eagles of Kefalonia wheeling above him!

But it was push on and push on, whatever the pain. And finally, when he had nothing more to give – there across the road was an open space. It had to be Regent's Park. He crossed the road, and was met by railings. How was he to get into the place? But taking a chance, going left rather than right, he followed the railings round until – *Thank you, St Gerasimos!* – there was the entrance, opening on to a space as wide as the Argostoli lagoon.

There were several different paths, but he took the one straight ahead, and heard the roaring of a lion and the high squawk of jungle birds as he ran on and on – until he heard the welcome sound of shouting and clapping, and whistles being blown.

He followed the sounds and took a left turn, then a right at a fountain – and there they were: the Regent's Park football pitches. He'd made it!

But it didn't look as if a Cup Final was being played here. Makis had imagined seeing twenty-two players on a pitch surrounded by a crowd of people. But here, the crowd was not of people but of pitches. They were all over this part of the park – and there seemed to be a team in red on nearly every one of them.

He ran down between the touch-lines looking for familiar faces, but he knew it was too late. All the games had started; and although later on players might have to come off because they were injured, or were sent off by the referee, no one else was ever allowed to go on. A game started with eleven players and those first eleven were the only people allowed to play the match, even if it ended up with eleven players against four.

So Denny Clarke would be playing in Makis's place, wearing his old dyed-red vest.

Makis ran down one side of a pitch, across behind the goals of two other games that were back to back – and suddenly he spotted one of the old red Imeson Street vests. He ran towards the game, but when he got there, the player wearing the vest wasn't Denny Clarke; it was a younger boy who sometimes took part in the playground games: Lennie Rainbird. Makis looked at the faces of the other players wearing the new red shirts. They were puffing and straining in a fast, hard-tackling game, with the defence trying to cover for Lennie Rainbird who was chasing around, as erratic as an eaglet. Makis knew that if David Sutton shouted 'W' or 'M', Lennie would have no idea what to do. It was clear that, had Makis or Denny Clarke been there, they would have made a big difference to the way the game was going. So where was Denny Clarke?

'Give me that shirt, lad!'

Mr Hersee jumped out at Makis from a group of people along the touchline. No, 'Where have you been?' No, 'Why are you late?' He grabbed at Makis's bag and pulled out the Imeson Street school shirt, spilling Makis's boots and shin pads on to the grass in an angry yank.

'Referee! Shirt change!' the headmaster shouted, when the ball went out of play: and before the throw-in was taken, the shirt was pulled over Lennie Rainbird's head. And when Makis looked closely, he could see that Lennie was playing in his street shoes

– and all because Makis Magriotis and Denny Clarke hadn't shown up for the match.

For a minute or so, Makis wondered whether to stay or go. Judging by the looks he got from the grim-faced Imeson Street players, he certainly wasn't welcome there. And as he watched the other team rob Rainbird and go on to score a goal, Costas Kasoulides ran to the touchline and shouted, 'Traitor!'

Makis trailed off home, a lion from the depths of the zoo roaring him on his way – to spend a most unhappy weekend, not even playing well on Sunday for Mr Laliotis. The violinist consoled him with a musicians' excuse: 'Some days the naughty fingers disobey the brain. It happens.' They cut the rehearsal short; but Makis knew he had disappointed the man.

While Makis's mother was out at the corner shop buying flowers, Makis had a chance to dig out *The Man Who Ran to Sparta* and throw it into the dustbin, burying it beneath a heap of dead coals.

Good riddance!

Chapter Fourteen

That Monday, Makis got to school as late as he could – he knew how unwelcome he would be in the playground. He wasn't the player who'd had his hand shaken by Mr Hersee any more.

And he was right. Freddie Gull spat in his direction. Lining up to go in, it was all elbows in the ribs and kicked shins, and 'Greek' seemed to be the swearword of the day. Makis knew without doubt that Imeson Street had lost in the Cup Final. But it wasn't until the school went in for assembly that he heard the score and realised how they'd lost. The boys who had played were paraded and clapped, and the result was given out: nil-one. The Reds had lost by that one goal scored from Lennie Rainbird's mistake. Makis not being there had made a difference.

But Lennie was praised by Mr Hersee for being 'one of our valiant heroes'.

When the team went back to their places in the hall, two other names were called out, and both boys were made to stand up in their lines: Makis Magritis and Dennis Clarke.

Makis stood, and not knowing where to look, he stared at the picture of the new Queen of England hanging up behind the headmaster. He stared at Elizabeth the Second until his tears dissolved her.

'Standing among you, like Judas trees in a vineyard, are two boys who are alone in their Imeson Street disgrace. Can you imagine Stanley Matthews of Blackpool not turning up for the Cup Final at Wembley? Can you imagine Nat Lofthouse telling his Bolton team-mates, "I fancied a lie-in, so I didn't bother getting up to join the team coach?" Imagine...' Mr Hersee was working himself up; he had to stop for a moment, and swallow. 'I can't imagine that happening, can you?'

The juniors shook their heads, and the infants chanted, 'No-o-o.'

'Well, Clarke and Magritis, these two,' – Mr Hersee pointed at the disgraced boys like a preacher from a street pulpit – 'these vipers in the bosom did just that on Saturday. Although honoured by being picked as first reserve, Clarke didn't even turn up at the field of play. And Magritis decided he'd got blanket fever and showed up too late to start the match – leaving brave, heart-as-big-as-his-chest Leonard Rainbird to throw himself into the fray.'

Makis felt dislike rising from the floor of the hall like the stink of seaweed, and sensed the teachers down the sides nodding and shaking their heads. But he could see nothing, standing with his head bowed – not with shame, but with the anger of injustice welling up inside him. This was not fair. Had Hersee bothered to ask him why he'd reached Regent's Park late? No! Did the headmaster know the state of his mother that Saturday morning? Would he even have understood her pain at seeing a picture in a book that looked just like her husband in his death agony? Did anyone in England care that a terrible earthquake had killed hundreds of people on his island in one minute?

Stirred in with his anger was not having the courage to shout something at the man at the other end of the hall. But perhaps that was just as well, because it would only have come out as a breathless snivel, his voice somewhere up in the ceiling beams.

So he stood there until he was ordered to sit down, and people shuffled away from him on each side – the start of isolation and insult that were to poison his day.

Denny Clarke was the worst. At morning playtime, as the football match went on around them, he grabbed Makis's neck. 'You dirty Greek traitor!' He pushed Makis and nearly floored him. 'You proper got me into trouble, you foreigner!'

'You not there, too!' Makis managed to get out.

'Wasn't playing, was I, Greekie? Waste o' time. Then you don' come – an' make me look as stinky as you!'

'That your problem, not my problem.'

Clarke got hold of Makis's jumper and pulled him violently towards him, stopping just short of a head-butt. 'I'll tell you your problem, you rotten turd. Me! I'm your problem! A'ter school, round Prince's – I'm gonna knock seven bells outa you, where Hersee an' no one can't stop me. An' you be there – if you got the guts.' He twisted a foot behind Makis's leg and pushed him hard, sending him down flat on his back on the tarmac. 'Prince's, a'ter school – an' bring your fightin' fists with you, if you got any.'

With a kick in the calf, Clarke went off – and Makis

picked himself up, hurting and choking in the throat with the rotten unfairness of life.

He didn't go to Prince's Fields after school. He didn't fight Denny Clarke. He went in the opposite direction, home to Georgiana Street, full of bile and unable to breathe properly in fury and frustration, his eardrums thumping with the beat of his heart. Even the earthquake that had killed his father and destroyed his Kefalonia life hadn't brought this burning turmoil inside him.

'What's the matter, Makis?' his mother wanted to know.

'Nothing.'

'Did the school lose their football match?'

She was sharp. Makis had to tell her that he hadn't got there in time on Saturday.

'You look different, Makis.'

'Well I'm not, I'm the same.'

It was a relief when Mr Laliotis came down to invite him upstairs for a rehearsal. And somehow that evening, against the odds, he was back to being a mandolin player. It was as if St Gerasimos had decided that not every part of his life was going to go wrong. Besides, he had to be good at the Acropolis on Saturday. It was why he had let himself seem a coward to Denny Clarke.

'If you want me to tell you that was good, Makis, I will tell you so – that was *very* good. Old men will cry.' The musician patted the back of Makis's hand. 'But please, use just a little less plectrum and a little more dripping of Assos honey across the bridging chords...'

Makis played a chord, to show how he could do honey.

'My boy! I applaud you.' And Mr Laliotis span his balalaika around to pat its back. 'Oh, Saturday is going to be so good...'

Mr Laliotis should have brought some calm to Makis. But that night in bed, he couldn't get the bitter taste of unfairness out of his mouth. And when he went to sleep, his dreams led him into a distressing place.

He went to the hall at Imeson Street school, with all the classes sitting in their assembly lines, staring at him as he stood out at the front. Again, he was in tears, his head bowed, his hot hands clenching and unclenching – because of what was being said.

'This boy has shamed us. He has shamed me, and he has shamed you. What was asked of him? What honourable action was he asked to do for the school? And what did he take upon himself to do instead?'

Makis could see the cold faces staring at him – even the infants at the front looked at him like enemies.

'He was asked,' the voice went on, 'to ooze honey from his strings, and not to cut across them as if his plectrum was a broken roof tile.'

Again, Makis could sense the teachers nodding as if they knew the difference.

'But did he? Could he?' – the rising voice came to a climax. 'No! He played with crude force, like Dennis Clarke hitting someone in the face!'

There was a pause, as the man at the front raised his hand like a conductor for the whole school to boo and boo. But it wasn't Mr Hersee standing there – it was Mr Laliotis, a man Makis thought of as a friend, who was treating him now with derision. It shocked him, and it hurt.

And that night, for the first time since he had been a very small boy back in Alekata, Makis woke from his nightmare in a wet bed. So, to his anger and his frustration, now he had to add his shame.

Chapter Fifteen

Next morning, Makis made his bed quickly, in the hope that his mother wouldn't find out how far away he was from taking his father's place in the home. He ate hardly any breakfast and got out of the house as soon as he could. In case anyone was watching, he turned the first corner as if he was going to school. But did he want to go to a place where he'd be treated like a traitor all day? That school was a place filled with people who didn't understand how plans can suddenly get upset. When those hateful people were pupils, that was one thing. But when they were teachers, too – who were supposed to know about helping you to learn things, and to grow up a good person – then everything was rotten.

So why not go and lose himself in Regent's Park – and stay there until his mother told the police, and they told the school, and everyone felt sorry for him instead of hating him? Or – a really stupid thought – why not go to the zoo and get eaten by a lion? Or how about finding the port where the ships came in from Greece, and stowing away on one that was flying the blue-and-white flag? Then he could go back to Kefalonia and Alekata, and build a small house from fallen stones, and patch up a boat and become a fisherman like his father. There were still people in Kefalonia who ate fish, weren't there?

But while he was having these thoughts – the possible, the stupid, and the wild – his feet were taking him the familiar way to school. His pride wouldn't let him run away. Makis Magriotis was not going to act as if he was ashamed of himself, nor as if he was afraid of Denny Clarke. Hold his head up high – that's what he was going to do.

He came to the school gate, and taking a deep breath, he went through it.

'Ere 'e 'is! The Greek coward! Couldn't stand an' fight like an Englishman!' This was Clarke.

'Don't go near to him – he stinks of goats!' This

was Costas Karoulides, back to his old insult.

'Traitor!' This was an infant, who wouldn't even know what the word meant.

But worse than the insults was what most other people did – they didn't speak to him, but bumped and bored into him as if he wasn't even there.

Makis's pride quickly drowned. But it wasn't too late to run off and do one of those other things he'd been thinking about, was it? The whistle hadn't blown yet. All he had to do was walk over to the gate and go through it.

Well, he would do that. He quickly turned to go, before the teachers came out to get everyone in.

But what was this? *Who* was this, striding into the playground with a mean and angry look on her face, and carrying the blackened copy of *The Man Who Ran to Sparta*?

'Where is he? The Principal?' his mother asked in Greek. She grabbed his hand and yanked him towards the school building. 'Makis – the Principal. Show me where he is!'

Makis knew the others in the playground were watching her, all saying things behind their hands and pulling faces. She wasn't waiting for his answer; she could see the door into the school and she started marching him towards it.

'Mama! Stop! What are you doing?'

But she pulled him in through the door, just as the teachers were coming out. The stares they gave one another were just like those Alekata warning looks of earthquake tremors to come. Trouble.

'Where?'

Makis could do nothing but take his mother along the corridor to the door she wanted. *Mr A.W. Hersee. Headmaster.* It was half-open. She knocked on it and stood waiting, her face frozen in determination.

'Yes?' Mr Hersee opened the door wider, saw Makis, and realised who this woman was. 'Ah.'

Makis could see him making an instant decision about the way he'd treat this mother. He could go into a rant about her son, the Cup Final traitor, or he could calmly explain to her his headteacher's duty to point out Makis's faults. He chose the second. 'Ah,' he said again, 'I think we must talk...' as if he'd sent for her to come.

'In!' Makis's mother said, in English. She pushed Makis into the head's room. She shut the door behind them, firmly.

'And how can I...?' In the face of Makis's mother's determination, Mr Hersee was shifting like a wind-change on water.

'See!' All the way from Georgiana Street Sofia Magriotis must have had her finger keeping a place in the page showing the terrible picture of the suffering runner. She cracked the book open and held it in the headteacher's face. 'See, Makis Dad, see!'

'Ah. Philippides...'

She pointed at Makis, and at the face in the picture. 'Dad. Makis's Dad.'

'A runner? Your father's an Olympic runner?' Mr Hersee asked Makis.

'Dead!' Makis's mother gave the universal sign for death, fingers drawn across her throat. 'Dead,' she went on, still in English. 'The earthquake,' she said in Greek – and looked at Makis for him to translate, which he did in such a soft voice that she had to prod him to say it again, louder.

'Sofia Magriotis see face look,' she said. 'Makis Dad. Dead Dad. Sofia very bad.' She mimed a fainting, a crying, a sort of collapse. 'I see. I see dead, in this.' She thumped herself in the chest. 'Sofia Magriotis very bad.'

'Ah.' Mr Hersee had an *ah* for every situation. This 'ah' said he was beginning to understand. 'Are we talking about Saturday?'

119

'Makis.' She patted Makis on the head. 'Makis' – she searched for the words – 'Good boy! Makis good boy for Mama!' she said triumphantly.

Mr Hersee turned to Makis, the look on his face distantly related to a smile. 'Your mother was bad, and you helped her…'

'Makis help. See Makis help.'

'Ah.' A full grasp now.

Makis took the book from his mother. 'I teach my mother reading. The face, she thinks – like my father. He dies under earthquake houses, look like this. She is bad. She is very bad…'

'And you felt you had to help her? You stayed till she recovered. This was what made you late…?'

'Yes.'

'You've been teaching her English? English,' he repeated to Makis's mother, smiling seriously, and nodding. 'You learn… English?'

'Ten green bottles,' she told him, to prove it.

'Ah.' Mr Hersee's face softened as he looked at Makis. 'And you missed the bus…?'

'I get lost,' Makis said. 'I run fast. I get lost.'

'Of course. But you turned up, didn't you? You got there too late – but, credit due…'

'Yes.'

But Sofia Magriotis wasn't finished. 'Makis bad – in this.' She knocked on Makis's forehead with a knuckle. 'Not good. Not Makis.' She mimed Makis's unhappiness with a face from a tragedy. 'He even wet the bed,' she said in Greek – her hands urging Makis to translate.

'We're not telling him that!' Makis said.

'Why didn't you say anything, lad?' The headteacher was waving his head this way and that as if in time to music. 'I'm not an unreasonable man. I wouldn't have said what I did to the school had I known the circumstances.' He turned to Makis's mother. 'In my ignorance of the true situation I made the situation worse, bad for Makis. I apologise. I'm sorry. Me' – he pointed both long-fingered hands towards his chest – 'very sorry.' And he nodded his sorrow like a priest at a graveside.

'Yes,' said Sofia Magriotis. 'Are you all right?' she asked Makis in Greek.

In truth, he wasn't sure whether he was or wasn't. He was proud of the way she'd stood up for him against Mr Hersee, *and* in a foreign language. But this sort of thing had never happened before, and it was embarrassing.

'Yes, I'm all right,' he told her.

'Truly?'

He nodded.

'I go. See me go.' And, leaving the dirtied reader on Mr Hersee's desk, she kissed Makis on the forehead and went out of the room, leaving headteacher and pupil standing there not looking at one another.

'Erm… You'd better get to your class, Magritis,' the man said. 'And I think we'll say nothing about the damaged book.' And between finger and thumb he dropped it into the waste basket.

Makis went out, his head in a daze. But one thing was clear – his mother was over her aftershock!

Chapter Sixteen

No more was said about it at home. That night Makis's bed was dry with fresh sheets, and the *Robin Hood* book was on the table – for going through again when they both felt ready. Makis wondered if this was something they might have to read over and over, because getting the next books home would be harder now that his secret teaching was known.

But whenever he wasn't busy doing something, the image that kept coming into Makis's head was of Denny Clarke – who was starting to look less like a fish and more like a bull. Mr Hersee had based his Tuesday morning assembly on Makis's Saturday – The Misunderstood Boy, and How First Appearances Can Bear False Witness. This meant that the finger of judgement was now pointed at Dennis Clarke, who had no excuse for letting down the school.

Even worse, Clarke was still left out of playground football, while Makis had been let back in.

'Coward Greek! Smarmy little beggar – getting yer mum up the school. Wait till I punch your 'ead off!'

'I fight,' Makis told him. 'Sunday.'

'Oh, Sunday! Goin' to church first to book your grave?'

'Sunday,' Makis repeated. 'Prince's Field. Eleven.'

'Yeah – an' you won' see twelve!'

All of which stayed in Makis's head – ringing like an ominous bell.

He could forget it for a bit when he was with Mr Laliotis – who was critical of his playing, but kind. Every evening now – except when Mr Laliotis was performing with a BBC orchestra – Makis spent an hour with him working on 'To Taste the Assos Honey'. The musician was professional and courteous, not at all the spiteful figure of Makis's nightmare; and they brought their duet to such a standard that they heard, 'Well done! Well done!' coming from Mrs Laliotis in the kitchen. Makis began to look forward to the coming Saturday.

Except that Saturday was to be followed by Sunday...

The Acropolis was a small Greek restaurant in Camden High Street, It put Makis in mind of the Mandolino. At one end of the roomful of old wooden tables and rush-seat chairs there had been a similar platform on which the musicians performed. On special nights, Makis's father and other Mandolino men had sat in a circle on the platform, facing in towards each other, playing and singing Kefalonian songs – voices in harmony, with guitar, mandolin, balalaika, and accordian. Here in the Acropolis, though, the chairs were set in a line for the performers to face the audience.

Sofia and Makis arrived with Mr and Mrs Laliotis, Makis carrying his Gibson the way his father would have done to walk to the village feast day, its case on a strap and slung over his shoulder. He saw his mother look into the room – at men in dark jackets with white open-necked shirts, women with immaculate hair, silky dresses and lace shawls, plates and cutlery set out, the Greek flag on the wall at the back of the platform – and she stopped in the doorway, putting her hand to her mouth. For a few seconds she was back in another country.

'We are sitting here.' Mrs Laliotis led them to a table at the front, below the platform. Makis's nervousness suddenly hit him in the stomach. Forget Denny Clarke. Nothing could get the heart thumping as hard as this: he, Makis Magriotis, was going to perform a duet with a musician from a BBC orchestra. And what frosted Makis's skin was his mother being there. From sitting crying in her bedroom a few weeks ago, here she was at the Acropolis looking as fine and elegant as any woman in the place. Mr Laliotis pulled a chair out for her to sit, and now she truly looked like someone who belonged.

People were still arriving, and recorded *rebetiko* music was playing, songs sung by the famous bazouki and singing pair Vassilis Tsitsanis and Marika Nimou. And Makis saw something he'd almost forgotten; men swinging and catching their *komboli* worry-beads, the way his father had done when he was relaxing with other men in the village. Where were those beads? Makis wondered. Probably buried with his father's body in the cemetery. Well, he could do with a string right now to help steady his nerves!

The Acropolis food was good, served buffet-style in stainless steel dishes: *stifádho*, *pastítsio*, meatballs, *moussakás*, *tzatzíki*, cucumber, courgettes, salads and *féta* cheese; but Makis just picked at a piece of bread. Mr and Mrs Laliotis didn't eat much either. Perhaps, Makis thought, that's how musicians always are before a performance. But at last the music began, provided by a quartet of guitar, mandolin, bazouki and accordion-playing – on their own as well as backing the singers – although this was no men's choir as there had always been in the Mandolino. This was men and women, and some of the songs were from Cyprus. Throughout the first half of the concert Makis's body felt lighter and lighter, his head like a helium balloon. When the time came, would he have the strength to even hold his plectrum?

Finally, Mr and Mrs Laliotis were introduced. To great applause they went up on to the platform. The audience was relaxed but attentive – except Makis. He thought he was going to explode. His hands were hot and wet and shaking, and he had to keep testing his legs to see if they would hold him up when he was announced.

He knew the Laliotis part of the programme which was before his part – and as the audience called for encores, he felt worse and worse. Why couldn't he start, and get it over with? Wild thoughts of freedom in Regent's Park and a ship at the docks came into his head again. How far away was that door?

And then he saw his mother. She was nodding her head slightly, looking across the table at him with that confident smile she'd always had when it was Spiros Magriotis holding the Gibson, ready to play. But tonight it would be—

'Makis Magriotis!'

Mr Laliotis was introducing him. Makis pushed back his chair with a squeal from the floor, his hand holding tight to the mandolin's fret.

'A young friend from our tragic island of Kefalonia, welcomed into our community here in London.' Mr Laliotis looked around the room. 'Would you like me to ask him to play a song from his island, to finish our concert?'

The audience – especially Sofia Magriotis – made sure the applause went on until Makis had found his place on the platform; where he gave a hurried bow and sat down next to Mr Laliotis. As he settled, the musician took his mandolin from him and quickly tuned it to the atmosphere of the room. Makis quietly wiped the plectrum dry on his handkerchief. And with the mandolin back in his hands, the final piece began.

The balalaika introduction, a nod to Makis, and with a catch of his heart, Makis began to play the beautiful melody, 'To Taste the Assos Honey'. Like drizzled honey itself, together they played a verse, then the chorus, and in the hushed room – not a sound from cutlery or plate or glass – they played; and baritone and alto, they sang the words of Makis' sand Sofia's island song.

I cross the blue Ionian Sea,
the blue stripes flying at our stern,
but when my sands are running out
to Kefalonia I'll return
to taste the Assos honey.

There was silence as they finished. Looking out over the hall, Makis could see heads nodding and eyes being wiped. And then the whole hall stood to clap them. Makis stood, too, and bowed in time with Mr Laliotis.

'One more bow,' the musician muttered, which they gave. 'Stand straight and still.' They did. 'No encore. Walk off.' And to claps, whistles, and shouts of 'Bravo!' they carried their instruments from the platform. 'It's always best that they want more than want less,' Mr Laliotis whispered under his breath.

At their table, Makis's mother was still clapping, straight-backed and modest and proud. Her eyes were wet, but tonight more with joy than sorrow. She kissed Makis on the forehead, and breathed in deeply.

'Tonight you made the Gibson truly yours, Makis. I bless it, and I bless you.' She took the mandolin from him, stroked it where it was chipped, and gave it back.

And had it not been for a stabbing thought of Denny Clarke, Makis would have considered himself the happiest boy in the world.

Chapter Seventeen

Makis woke up feeling frightened. He heard his mother humming the Assos honey song in the kitchen, but he wanted to push past her and out into the yard to breathe some fresh air. His nerves the night before in the Acropolis had shown themselves in a lack of breath and freezing skin. But the fear of being hurt is different from any other fear. Imagining a pounding from Denny Clarke had all Makis's insides churning, and he felt that at any moment he might be sick.

Denny Clarke! This morning after Cathedral he was going to have to fight the boy – who was bigger all round than he was, and had fists like the rocks on Alekata beach. Makis looked at his own hands; his plectrum hand, and his fret hand. To some, he might have seemed a coward, but he had deliberately put off the fight long enough to keep those hands in condition for the concert with Mr Laliotis. But now they were going to be used for fighting.

He couldn't eat breakfast, hid his toast, and got ready for going to the Cathedral, keeping his eye on the mantelpiece clock. Two hours to pain – to his body hurting and his face looking like that picture of Phidippides at Sparta. Looking like his father had.

But at this sudden thought, out of nowhere a shaft of hope hit Makis, a glimmer of an idea. He'd learned more from his father than fishing and playing mandolin, hadn't he?

The time came, at last. Cathedral was over and their Sunday morning walk, with him silent and his mother with music on her tongue, was finished. He told her part of the truth – that he'd got to meet a boy and he'd be back later – and he ran off.

Prince's Fields didn't look the same place. This morning there was a dog being walked, and a father with his children and a brown-paper kite that wouldn't fly. The place was different, felt wrong.

And there, standing watching him from under a tree, was Denny Clarke!

Makis's heart raced as he walked over to him. He'd done nothing wrong to this boy. What Hersee had said about Clarke was to do with what Clarke himself had done. Makis's part of things had been a separate matter; but in his stupid, goat-headed way, Clarke wanted to feel better by fighting him.

'You come, then, Greekie?'

'I come.' Makis stood off from the boy, his fists clenched, ready.

'You gonna say sorry?'

Makis stared him in the sweaty face. No, Dennis Clarke wasn't a fish any more – he was a goat, a stupid goat.

'No!'

'I'm gonna kill you!'

'Kill,' Makis said. 'Try!' he added, bravely.

Out shot Clarke's right fist – the boy had a long reach and Makis hadn't backed off far enough. The punch caught him on the cheekbone and twisted his neck. And his feet wouldn't work, they were caught in the grass and he couldn't back-pedal.

Crack! Another punch hit him on the forehead and sent him flying backwards. And on came Clarke for another free punch because Makis couldn't reach him with his own flailing fists: his face was twisted, his head down – real boxer-style.

But what had Makis's father taught him, when a head-down goat like this came at him?

As Clarke's right fist came in, Makis caught his wrist, took the force of the punch in his arm muscles – the muscles that had wrestled some of the biggest goats in Alekata – and wouldn't let go. Clarke swung a left at him – and Makis dodged, couldn't quite grab that wrist and took another punch to the face. But with his left hand he held on desperately to Clarke's right wrist; and however the boy twisted, he couldn't get it free. And the next time, as Clarke's left came in again, Makis caught it. Now he had both wrists.

Head to head, face to face, they wrestled with their arms. Clarke's face said he didn't know how to deal with this. Would he kick next, or butt with his head? But Makis kept his head back and used the net-heaving strength in his arms to stay uppermost. Clarke swore and spat, but Makis held on and took the strain as the boy exhausted himself trying to get free or to aim a kick. But none of that worked for him, and with a sudden downward jerk, Makis pulled him off-balance, and used his old Alekata goat-wrestling memory to swing Clarke over, down, down, down on his right hand side – and thumped the boy to the ground. Makis jumped on top of him, like a Greek hero riding a Mount Ēnos stallion. Sitting high on Clarke's chest where his kicking legs couldn't help him, he pinned down both the boy's wrists to the grass.

Clarke could heave his backside, he could wriggle his torso, he could lift his head and try to free his arms – but he was pinned to the ground. There was no way he could get up unless Makis let him. Spiros Magriotis had taught his son well.

'Hey! Hey!' Makis shouted over to the man with his children. 'Come! Come!'

'Let me up, Greekie! Let me up, you little squirt!'

'Come!'

While Denny Clarke wriggled and squirmed, Makis held him there until the father with his children came over.

'Hello? What's going on here?'

'See!' Makis said. He had recognised the little girl when he'd come into the park. She was an infant from Imeson Street school who had sat in the front row during Mr Hersee's assemblies.

'Let go!' Clarke was shouting.

'Let him up, son,' the father said. 'He looks like he's had enough.'

But Makis only twisted his head up to the girl. 'See?' he asked. 'You see him? You see him on ground, Makis on top?'

'What's all this?' the father asked.

But the girl said, 'I see.'

Makis nodded into Clarke's face. 'She see!' he said. 'You talk me bad again. You want fight again – and she tell to boys at school.'

Clarke put his head on one side and tried to spit, but could only dribble.

'Now you get up.' Makis sprang off Clarke, and Clarke slowly got to his feet. He opened his mouth to say something; but he must have thought better of it, because he turned and ran out of Prince's Fields.

'You'd better get a steak on that face,' the father told Makis, 'or you're going to be black and blue tomorrow.'

'Thank you,' Makis said. And he ran off home.

Sofia was appalled. When Makis saw her looking at his face, he knew she was thinking of his father, lying there after the earthquake. 'What's happened?' she demanded. 'Who's done this to you?'

Makis pulled away from the handkerchief that was blotting at his face. And he smiled. 'I had a fight,' he said, 'with a boy who called me nasty names.'

'Did you hurt him?'

'I won. I wrestled him like I wrestled the big goats. He won't be saying those names again.'

'What names? What's he been saying?'

Makis stared his mother out. 'It doesn't matter,' he said. 'He won't say them any more.' He looked beyond her to the table where she had been sitting with paper and an envelope and a pen. 'Who are you writing to?'

She put a hand to the letter as if she was about to turn it over. But instead, she held it up in front of him. 'It's to Dimitris, your father's friend in the Mandolino choir – if he's still in Argostoli.' She took a breath. 'He didn't die, I know he didn't, I saw him afterwards, at the cemetery – and his house wasn't damaged so badly…'

Through a rapidly closing eye, Makis couldn't

quite read the writing on the letter. 'What are you saying to him?'

Sofia put the paper down again and faced Makis square on. It took a number of breaths before she could speak. 'I'm writing to ask him to send us the mandolin music for the songs your father used to sing. He might have them himself.'

Makis looked at her, and across at the Gibson that was hanging again on the living-room wall.

'Or he might be able to find them somewhere. The way you sang and played 'To Taste the Assos Honey' is more important than fighting a stupid boy, I can tell you. You are a Kefalonian, but Kefalonia isn't the island it was, not after the earthquake, not after so many died, and now that so many have left the island...'

Makis frowned. All this was true, but why was she saying it?

'...But a boy who can sing and play so well, can surely learn to sing and play all our Kefalonian music. And a boy who can teach his mother English could go back one day, when Argostoli has been rebuilt, to teach the island to sing its songs again.'

There were tears in her eyes; and there were tears in Makis's, too, which stung.

He said nothing for a long, long time – because he knew he wouldn't be able to get the words out without sounding like a bleating goat.

But at last he took a deep breath, and taking the Gibson down from the wall and stroking the chip on its body, he said, 'I think Papa would like that.'

BERNARD ASHLEY now writes full time after
a full career in teaching. He first went into print after
writing stories for children in his junior school class.
Before teaching, he served in the RAF – and he will
always be grateful for being taught to type instead of
learning to fly a Hawker Hunter! He has written
over fifty books of realistic fiction for young people
– from picture books to teenage novels – and has
been shortlisted for the Carnegie Medal three times.
His BBC TV serial *Dodgem* won a Royal Television
Society award for the best children's entertainment
of its year. He is a popular visitor to schools,
and enthuses about reading and writing at meetings
all over the UK. His first book for Frances Lincoln
was *Angel Boy*, followed by *Ronnie's War*.
Bernard lives in south London, only a street or two
away from where he was born.